Fielder's Choice

By A. Ganu

Dedications

I would like to extend a sincere Thank You to Chris Baty for developing the National Novel Writing Month concept. It has challenged me to get serious about having fun writing.

Another huge Thank You goes to Mary, the Central Iowa Authors Municipal Liaison for her tireless enthusiasm, cheerleading, and writer event planning which allowed me to complete this novel.

And to Ray Kurzweil, whose predictions about nanotechnology in the 2020's gave me the idea for this book.....

Fielder's Choice:

In baseball, fielder's choice is a term used to refer to a variety of plays involving an offensive player reaching a base due to the defense's attempt to put out another baserunner, or the defensive team's indifference to his advance. Fielder's choice is not called by the umpires on the field of play; rather, it is recorded by the official scorer to account for the offensive player's advance without crediting him with an offensive statistic such as a hit or stolen base.

"Fielder's Choice" Wikipedia: The Free Encyclopedia. Wikimedia Foundation, Inc. 27 April 2014. March 28 Mar. 2015.

For Brad Dickson, it has a different meaning altogether................

Chapter 1

"That leg is gonna take some time to heal," Al Simpson, in his 32nd year as trainer for the Detroit Tigers, was shaking his head and raising his eyebrows, "you are not a kid anymore Brad."

"How long do you think?"

"Don't know 'til the doc takes a look and we get an MRI, but I'm guessin' you're going on the 15-day for sure, maybe more, your season's probably finished."

"That jerk Rodriquez, there's no way he breaks up the DP."

"Shoulda been tossed."

"Tossed? Ross is a sissy, he don't have the guts to toss anyone."

"I've seen him toss guys out for a lot less. Maybe he was blocked out on the play, Brad."

"Yeah? Bull. Now I'm out and that lowlife isn't. He'll know what it feels like when he's my age."

"He'll never be your age," quipped Al, amusing himself at the expense of the Tigers' $35 million dollar a year superstar, as he picked up a couple of towels and headed out of the training room.

"Go screw yourself," Brad yelled at Al's back as the door shut behind him.

Brad sighed deeply and looked around the training room. He'd been spending a lot of time in here this season. It seemed every time he started to get his groove back, something would happen and set him back, put him out. And the stays on the disabled list were getting longer and more frequent. This would be the third time this year. Not like in the early days, when he could nurse an injury while still performing at a high level. He got banged up quite a few times and each time it didn't seem to bother his body at all. Just rub some dirt on it and get back out there; it's what his dad had always preached. He'd endured a lot of bumps, tweaks, sprains, and bruises, over his 14 year pro career. But lately, he'd been noticing the injuries took longer to heal. A little sprain would bother him for days. His muscles ached in the mornings and night games in cool weather were especially tough to get warmed up for. It took longer to loosen up, longer to cool down, longer to stretch, longer to do just about everything. He even noticed it at the plate. Sometimes, when he would get a good cut, there would be a sharp pain shoot down his left side and he had to grit his teeth to keep the pitcher, his fans, the reporters, and especially the owner, from seeing it. It seemed all the things he used to do with ease, without even thinking about it, had now become a chore. It seemed ages ago, way back in '24, last year, at the ripe old age of 36, when he won his most recent of 5 MVP titles.

"What the hell, I could use some time off anyway," he actually said out loud. Brad grabbed his towel and gingerly hopped off the table and headed for the shower room.

Chapter 2

"Whadda ya say, doc?"

"Well, Brad, it appears the intensity of the collision snapped your leg back to far, too fast, and you have pulled one of your quadriceps muscles, to be specific, the vastus lateralis," Dr. Lewis, the ball club's team doctor replied, rubbing his hand down the outer part of Brad's left thigh. And you are going to need a few months for it to recover, if it responds at all. That was quite an impact. Your leg was bent back very abruptly during the slide. It may end up and require surgery."

"I know doc, I've seen the film", deadpanned Brad. "Well that ain't gonna happen. The playoffs are in two weeks and I intend to be in it. We're in a dang fight here, doc." Brad always toned down his language for the doctor, and almost no one else.

"Sorry Brad, I understand, but you are in no shape to play. The muscle needs to heal. You will need to spend a minimum, and I say minimum, of three months off it, before you even think about getting the leg back into playing shape. You're not 20 years old, son."

"Don't call me son," Brad bristled at the condescending tone in the doctor's voice, "I'm Brad Dickson, and don't you forget it. Just give me a cort shot doc, and I'll be back in the lineup tomorrow."

"Sorry Brad, I'm trying to think about your future."

"Bullshit. You're just concerned with covering your own ass." Respect only went so far with Brad.

"Whatever you think Brad, I'm telling you, you are done for this year."

"No I'm not!" Brad hobbled out of the room.

"He's really in no shape to play again this year," Dr. Lewis said, now addressing Bob Startlin, the Tiger manager, and Mr. Yorkey, the owner of the team.

"Christ, that's all we needed," Bob said.

"You'll just have to tell the boys they need to step up," Albert Yorkey, the sole owner and self-made Internet billionaire said matter-of-factly, "that's what I pay YOU to do." He walked out of the room, leaving his manager staring at the back of his head.

Dammit, Yorkey thought to himself, walking down the long hallway leading to his opulent office, my zillion dollar diva has done it again. He grabbed the ball cap off his head, and slapped his leg hard with it. "I really need to figure out a way to dump this has-been, his best days are through," he mumbled as he threw the door open.

Marisa had immediately left her front row seat when they carried Brad off the field and had worked her way down to the clubhouse. She was sitting on a bench in the narrow hallway when the door opened and Brad hobbled out. He looked at her and for the first time, she saw the slightest hint of fear in his eyes.

"Hi baby, what's the word?" she said as she rose to give him a hug. He straightening up and drew back a little, just out of reach of her, not letting her wrap her arms around him. "That was a pretty cheap shot by Rodriquez."

"I'll be fine, no worries," he said, brushing past her, "just a little muscle pull, I'll be fine."

She detected the grimace as he spoke, and did not believe a word of it. "Yeah, right. What did the doctor say?"

Unable to bluff his way out of it and too tired to care, Brad replied, "he thinks I need rehab, stay off the leg, maybe surgery, but I just need to rest it tonight, maybe put some ice on it. I'm tellin ya, I'll be fine."

"Listen to me, Brad," she caught his arm and with force, stopped him cold in his tracks. "If Dr. Lewis says you need to rehab, then you need to do as he says. He's only looking out for your best interest. He's never lied to you before. You need to listen to him and do what he says."

"What I need is a drink, that's what I need."

Chapter 3

Brad awoke at 2 AM with a severe throbbing in his left leg. He lay awake trying to will the pain away, but the leg was not buying. After 30 minutes of wishing, hoping, he slowly slipped the bad leg out of bed and onto the floor. He brought himself up to a sitting position and tried to push off of the bed to rise, but the leg had no strength. He shifted his weight to the other leg, pushed down on the bed and rose up. The throbbing was intense now as the blood rushed through his damaged thigh muscle. Marisa stirred but did not see the agonized look on his face as he took a step on the leg. This is bad, he thought, this is very bad. He had never experienced pain this intense. With each beat of his heart, he could feel the cold steel blade of a knife thrust into his thigh, just above the knee. He grimaced with each step and limped his way into the bathroom, trying hard to not put any weight on the bad leg. He turned on the light and looked into the mirror. What he saw, he didn't like, His face was drawn and there were bags under his eyes.

"Jeez, I'm only 37 years old; I've got a lot left. I can't be done for the year, I just can't." He opened the medicine cabinet, grabbed the Advil bottle and shook 4 tablets into his hand. This will make it better, he thought, as he popped them into his mouth, ran some water in a glass, and washed down the pills.

After a couple of hours, Brad realized one thing; the pills did not make it better. He returned to bed, looked at the alarm clock on the bedside table and thought, crap, it's only 4 AM and I cannot go to sleep. Marisa rolled over and threw an arm around his chest, and snuggled closer.

"You OK, baby?"

"Sure, had to wizz. Go to sleep."

"Have you been up long?"

"No, just got up," he lied, hoping she would stop talking.

"How's the leg feel?"

"Pretty good. I think it's going to be fine."

She shifted a little and settled back into sleep. Brad lay on his back, hands folded behind his head, eyes wide open staring at the ceiling he could not see. "Just fine," he repeated, hoping it was true.

Somehow, despite the constant throbbing in his left leg, he must have drifted back to sleep because the next time he looked at the clock, it was 5 minutes until 8. Marisa was up, and he could hear her in the kitchen. Making pancakes, he hoped. A cupboard door slammed shut - the mixing bowl? Tinny rustling sounds - grabbing the spatula out of the utensil bowl? Refrigerator door opening and shutting - getting the milk out? He was sure she was whipping up his favorite breakfast meal, pancakes. She always made him pancakes after a loss, or a bad night at the plate. He'd been eating a lot of pancakes lately. Today she'd need to make a stack to the ceiling to fix this one.

He gingerly slid his left leg over the silk sheet and eased it to the floor. The throbbing had subsided a bit, but it was still excruciating to get the leg to follow his will. He lifted the right leg out and on to the floor and hoisted himself up.

After doing his morning nature call, trying to hide the limp, he gingerly walked to the kitchen and confirmed what he had suspected, Marisa was making blueberry pancakes. She had a stack of three ready to go and looked up at Brad as he entered the kitchen.

"How ya feeling baby?"

"A lot better. I don't think Doc Lewis knows what he's talking about to be honest."

"He's been your doctor for years, Brad," she insisted. "So I think he knows your body quite well."

"So do you, eh?" he said as he put his arms around her. "We'll see what the tests show. I'm sure I'll be in the lineup tonight."

"I hope you're right," she replied, wriggling out of his bear hug as she grabbed up his plate and set it on their dining room table.

They ate their breakfast in silence. Marisa had laid aside thoughts about Brad's leg and was now actually thinking about the shopping trip with her friends she had planned for the day, a trip it appeared she was probably going to miss. Brad was thinking about the MRI test later in the morning and getting the news. He was afraid it would be bad. His leg never throbbed like this before.

I don't need this at this time in my career, his thoughts focusing on his job. I'm the best player in baseball and everyone knows it. I just have to get in the game tonight. Maybe I'll get a chance to get even with Rodriguez, that jerk.

At 10 o'clock, Brad and Marisa walked through a side door of the Henry Ford Hospital, avoided the group of reporters in the lobby, made it to the elevator and rode it to the 6th floor. They were met by a nurse and Marisa walked into the empty waiting room as the nurse escorted Brad to the door of a dressing room.

"Please go in and take off your clothes and put on the gown provided. Put your clothes, watch and ring into the white tray on the bench and then put the tray into the locker," she growled, obviously unimpressed her charge was the most famous athlete in Detroit. "Lock the locker and when you are done, ring the buzzer on the wall there and I'll come in and take the key and escort you down to MRI. Do you have any questions, Mr. Dickson?"

"Nope," Brad said harshly, "I've done this more times than you have lady."

She left him alone and Brad stripped down and stepped into the threadbare gown. He had to twist the MVP ring somewhat to get it off his finger, but it finally popped off. He put the ring and his watch into the tray and set it into the locker. He hung his shirt and pants on a hanger and hooked it onto the bar in the locker. Brad shut the door, turned the key and pulled it out. He looked over at the buzzer, gave a big sigh and pushed the button.

The nurse was there in an instant and reached out for the key.

"Don't lose that key, and don't even think of looking in there," he barked, "there's a ring and a watch in the locker and it better be there when I'm done."

"It will be Mr. Dickson," she said sweetly with a big toothy fixed smile on her face, with the "you conceited creep" left unspoken.

She led Brad down a long hallway. The MRI test room was on the right. They turned in and were greeted by the technician.

"Hi Mr. Dickson, I'm David. I will be conducting your MRI this morning. I will need you to lay down on the table and skooch up as far as you can with your head near the top of the hood. When the testing starts, you will be moved into the...."

"I know, I know. Let's get on with it."

The technician glanced over at the nurse, who was standing near the door. She flashed her best plastic smile at David, rolled her eyes, and escaped from the room.

Dr. Reynolds, the radiologist, was in the MRI exam room now, "Brad, I know you've been through this before but I have to ask you some questions before we begin."

"Knock yourself out, doc."

Dr. Reynolds' questions and Brad's answers followed the same script they had many times, and when they were done with the ritual, Dr. Reynolds picked up an IV catheter from the cart and said, "Brad, this solution contains Gadolinium. It is a metal used to get a better picture of the damage to your muscle. We've never used this method before with you, but I feel with the damage you've sustained, we need to get the best possible view of your quad. We usually like to use an arthrographic procedure, where we inject the contrast fluid directly into the muscle, but we do not

14

want to injure it any more than what is already done, so I will instead use an IV. We will first run a series of tests. After that initial set, we will add the Gadolinium to your IV drip, and repeat the tests again. These two sets will give us a baseline and a detailed view of your quadriceps. You may feel a slight burning sensation when the contrast material is added, but it will quickly subside as the solution traverses your body. It will add a few minutes to the test time, but we should have you out of here in about 45 minutes. Do you have any questions before we get started?"

"Just do it, Doc."

Dr. Reynolds nodded at the technician, who pushed a button and the slab Brad was laying on slowly moved into the MRI machine.

"Good luck, Brad."

Soft music was playing inside the cylinder and Brad closed his eyes, trying to relax.

"Try to relax, Mr. Dickson."

Brad smiled to himself.

Outwardly he appeared calm, but the reality was he got unnerved every time he'd had this test done. Generally, Brad was not claustrophobic, but he did not like being inside the MRI. He did not like the loud humming of the machine as the magnetic field pulsed, on and on pulsing and humming louder and louder and it seemed like it would continue forever.

After an eternity, the humming and pulsing abruptly stopped. Brad's overloaded senses began to calm. He opened his eyes and realized he was still in the long tube. He felt his body slowly reversed out of the machine and he was once again in the presence of Dr. Reynolds and the technician. Dr. Reynolds started the IV in Brad's arm, and after seeing the drip start, added the Gadolinium. Brad felt a sudden flushing which just as quickly, subsided. A few moments passed, when Dr. Reynolds removed the IV and David rolled Brad back into the big white donut. This time, he was more relaxed than before. The loud banging of the machine did not seem to rattle him as much and he was sure the time in the tube was not nearly as long.

Brad was again rolled out and helped off the table by David, who escorted him to the changing room. He hurriedly got into his clothes, put on his jewelry, threw the wadded up gown into a corner and limped out of the room. As he passed the waiting room, he motioned toward Marisa to get up and left the MRI as fast as his gimpy leg would allow.

Chapter 4

The news had not been good. Severe tear of the vastus lateralis, as Dr. Lewis had diagnosed. Surgery recommended immediately. Off the leg for 6 weeks, Six to nine months rehab.

Brad limped over to the refrigerator, grabbed a beer and flopped down on the couch. The beer was gone in one long pull. Brad threw the empty can across the room.

"You can't solve it that way," Marisa said, picking up the empty can, "you'll have to be patient, baby."

"Get me another beer and leave me alone."

"I won't leave you alone. You need to do what they say and get on with it," she said as she handed him a second beer.

"Get on with it, huh? Nine months rehab? I'm 37 frickin' years old. I don't have nine months to rehab. This is the last year of my contract. If I can't play, I won't have anything to negotiate with for next season."

"You need to accept it baby and get on with it, like I said. The sooner the better."

"Easy for you to say, huh? You got it easy, just living the good life spending all of Brad's money. What are you going to do when that gravy train doesn't leave the station?"

He downed the second beer faster than the first.

"You know that's not true Brad. I'm with you forever." Not wanting to go down that road any further, she added, "Anyway,

I've got to get going. I need to pick up my mom. We're going shopping for some drapes for her. Can I get you anything else before I leave?"

"Another beer," he said, lifting himself off the couch and headed towards the refrigerator.

"I'll be home in a couple of hours. Try to relax and get some rest." She grabbed the keys to the Mercedes, and opened the door.

"Bring me back a new leg," he called to her as the door shut.

Alone, Brad looked down at his injured leg. I can't let this end my season. What I need is to get another MVP, I need to win the batting title, I need another World Series ring, and I need to be admired by every hot chick in this country.

He finished the third beer and walked over to his desk and turned on the computer. When it finally finished booting up, he brought up the search engine.

He typed in MUSCLE SURGERY. 109 million results! Muscle injuries, bone and muscle surgery, muscle strain treatment. He scrolled through numerous pages, not finding anything exciting.

He cleared the search window and tried QUADRICEP INJURY. A little better, only 134,000 results. He spent some time reading about partial and complete tears. Most entries were about contusions, not tears. He tried again, QUADRICEP TEAR INJURY. He clicked on the first entry. He scrolled through the Cause and Symptoms sections, unconsciously nodding as he skimmed over the definitions. When he got to the Treatment section, he took his hand off the mouse and began to read carefully. He frowned at the screen when reading the nonsurgical

18

treatment was usually the case with small tears. But the injury he had would require surgery, as he had been told. A new type of procedure using suture anchors would eliminate drill holes in his kneecap, but still require months of rehab. The prospects did not look good, to say the least. Another website touted BFST. That sounds good, he thought, Blood Flow Stimulation Therapy. He had heard of it. One of the younger guys had used it a couple years ago to get back from a calf injury. It took 3 or 4 weeks, he remembered. "I don't have 3 or 4 weeks", he murmured finishing his thought.

Dejected, he typed MIRACLE QUALRICEP INJURY TREATMENT". Now we're getting somewhere, only a few thousand results. More BFST hits. One guy posted a webpage touting the benefit of doing cortisone shots instead of surgery. "It healed fine after awhile", was the testimonial. What an idiot, Brad thought.

He scrolled down through a couple of pages of similar hits. I need something that's going to work NOW.

The beer was helping to feed his imagination; next he tried FUTURE CURES FOR QUAD INJURY. He started talking to the screen, "this looks interesting, bio therapy". He read aloud, "using bio-medicine to develop tissue to reconstruct tendons and muscles. This treatment is available to totally reconstruct an injured quadriceps in less than three months."

"Damn!"

Next he typed BIO CURES FOR QUADS. Scrolling through the results he saw: stem cell treatment, Nano biotechnology, injected glucosamine.

"Whaaaat?"

Brad scrolled back up. "Nano biotechnology? What the hell is that?"

He clicked on the first entry, the Wiki definition:

"This discipline helps to indicate the merger of biological research with various fields of nanotechnology. Concepts that are enhanced through nanobiology include: nanodevices, nanoparticles, and nanoscale phenomena that occurs within the disciple of nanotechnology. This technical approach to biology allows scientists to imagine and create systems that can be used for biological research. Biologically inspired nanotechnology uses biological systems as the inspirations for technologies not yet created. We can learn from eons of evolution that have resulted in elegant systems that are naturally created.

The most important objectives that are frequently found in nanobiology involve applying nanotools to relevant medical/biological problems and refining these applications. Developing new tools for the medical and biological fields is another primary objective in nanotechnology. New nanotools are often made by refining the applications of the nanotools that are already being used. The imaging of native biomolecules, biological membranes, and tissues is also a major topic for the nanobiology researchers. Other topics concerning nanobiology include the use of cantilever array sensors and the application of nanophotonics for manipulating molecular processes in living cells."

Further down the entry, he clicked on "The Nanobiology Imperative." He read about nanofactories, the merging of nanotechnology and biology. A Dr. Rasheesh Gupta had received a patent in 2021 for the creation of nanorobots which had successfully repaired tissue in laboratory mice. The nanobots, as they were called in the article, had been programmed with the test mice's own DNA sequence and coded to generate specific tissue based on the repair being made. Dr. Gupta had successfully regenerated tissue in these mice.

Brad quickly back clicked to the search engine screen and typed:

DR. RASHEESH GUPTA

Over 300,000 results were returned.

He quickly clicked on the first one, a news story about the trials leading up to the issuing of Dr. Gupta's first patent for nanobots that were injected into the mice's bloodstream and removed potential blockages by finding deposits of cholesterol and separating the LDL lipids from the HDL lipids and further breaking down the LDL into harmless proteins that were then washed from the blood vessel by the blood flowing through the mice's veins.

He returned to the list and scrolled down through it. On the third page, he found a link titled: "Dr. Gupta, On the Brink of Immortality?"

Brad's curiosity was stoked; he clicked on the link and read:

"Early this month, Dr. Rasheesh Gupta, distinguished scientist and doctor, announced his company, The Gupta Institute of Nano Robotics, of Chicago, Illinois, had a breakthrough in their reconstruction lab. The lab conducts research on the ability of nanobots to mine, or harvest, chemicals in the body of mice to use for rebuilding certain cells, based upon the instructions given to them in their programming. Dr. Gupta acknowledged his lab was able to completely repair a broken shoulder in a mouse in 4 days. The announcement comes on the heels of a number of claims the company has made in the past few months of progressively faster times to reconstruct body parts in laboratory experiments. When asked when and if the experiments will have practical application, Dr. Gupta replied "no comment". The AMA, FDA as well as the Consumer Product Safety Commission all have investigations open as to the validity of the company's claims."

Brad read on about how the doctor, having graduated from MIT with doctorates in medicine and engineering had established himself as the preeminent expert of nanobiotechnology. Where he had developed nanobot processes in laboratory animals, starting with simple skin cells in mice, progressing through kidney and stomach cell regeneration and most recently had been running experiments to regenerate muscle and cartilage tissue. Brad found out the Institute was privately funded, and was unable to find out much more about the company or their current research and projects. He did a Google map search for Nano Robotics in Chicago and found it was located on Campbell Park Drive, near the University of Illinois Chicago Medical Center. He jotted down the address and phone number, logged off and shut down his PC.

22

He grabbed his cellphone, stared at it, set it down and got up to get a beer. In the kitchen, he paced, being reminded each time he put weight on his bad leg that he had a great need and desire to fix his wounded leg.

Can the doctor help me? Can he get me back in the game? At all? Before the playoffs? Now?

He reached for his phone again, punched in the first few numbers then put it to sleep again and set it down. When he finished his beer, he grabbed the phone once more took a deep breath, focused on the keypad and dialed the number.

"Nano Robotics, how may I direct your call?" came the friendly but businesslike female voice.

"This is Brad Dickson; I'd like to speak to Dr. Gupta."

Not recognizing his name, the receptionist said, "I'm sorry Mr. Dickson, Dr. Gupta does not take unsolicited calls. Does this pertain to a previous contact with Dr. Gupta?"

"No, Miss, I read about some of his work and I'm interested in talking to him about it."

"What news agency are you with? I will tell you up front that Dr. Gupta does not give interviews."

"No ma'am, no agency, I'm a professional baseball player, and I would like to talk to the doctor about a personal matter."

"Sir, Dr. Gupta does not treat athletes", she stated with firmness, starting to get agitated with this obtrusive caller, and added as sarcastically as she could, "Dr. Gupta's research is for the betterment of mankind to help cure real and serious problems."

Usually Brad would have explained to this woman how important he was and she wasn't, but continued to play nice, because he REALLY wanted to talk to the good doctor.

"Miss, I'm not necessarily looking for treatment, I just have a couple of things I'm curious about and would like to ask Dr. Gupta about them. What harm could there be in that?"

"Well, I'm afraid it's not possible", she snapped back, desperate to get this jock off the phone. "If you must, you could mail a letter with your questions and be sure to include a self-addressed stamped envelope or you will get no response. One of Dr. Gupta's colleagues will respond to your questions within a few days."

Brad had enough, "Listen lady, you obviously don't know anything about baseball, or else you would know I'm the reigning MVP of all of baseball and I really need to talk to the doctor. It's of the utmost importance."

"Do you play for the Cubs?"

"Of course not, I play for the Detroit Tigers."

"Oh, too bad. Send the letter and someone will get back to you. Good day sir."

He heard a click, looked at the cell phone face and realized the call had ended.

"That bitch", he yelled, throwing the phone across the room, shattering it into many non-working pieces.

He walked to the wall phone, thumbed through the Rolodex on the counter and dialed. When the call was answered, he said "get me

24

on a flight to Chicago in the morning", and replaced the phone in
its cradle.

Chapter 5

Brad landed at O'Hare at 12:22 PM the following day. Dragging his carryon, he hobbled through the terminal to the taxi stand. The cabbie, recognizing him said, "Good day Mr. Dickson, it will be a pleasure to serve you today", as he opened the door. Brad slid into the back seat. The cabbie hopped in and turned around, "Mr. Dickson, what an honor it is to have you in my cab. I'm a huge Tigers fan and you are my favorite."

"Thanks," Brad replied, already regretting the upcoming ride of incessant praise and undoubtedly, hundreds of questions, "3227 Campbell Park Drive".

"Yes sir, got a hot date there?" he inquired as they pulled away from the curb and into the airport traffic.

As he had feared, the cabbie jawboned the entire trip.

"The Tigers are looking good."

"Yes, we are."

"As long as the pitching holds up down the stretch. How many homers do you have now, 26?"

"27."

"Wow, that's more than last year?"

"No, last year I hit 52." Some fan, Brad thought.

"Do you think you'll get there again?"

"Of course."

"What place are the Tigers in?"

Does this guy follow the Tigers at all?

"We're a game and a half ahead of the Twins."

For 30 very long minutes, Brad put up with the interrogation until they mercifully pulled up at 3227 Campbell Park Drive.

Brad looked at the meter: $28.40. He pulled out two twenties and offered it to the cabbie. "Here, keep it." Happy the ride was over, he grimaced as he opened the door, turned out of the seat and did his best to hop out of the cab smoothly as to not give the cabbie cause to quiz him further. He looked up at the white 4 story windowless building then back at the cab and started walking.

Why is he going to that joint, the cabbie wondered, looking atop the building at the ten foot high aluminum sign: GUPTA INSTITUTE. "Good luck with the pennant race, Mr. Dickson."

Brad kept walking without acknowledgement.

The driver stuffed the bills in his shirt pocket, reset his meter and drove off. "What an arrogant dirtbag," he muttered aloud.

Brad painfully climbed the steps leading to the double doors, grabbed the handle, took a very deep breath and walked in.

The lobby of the building was plain and somewhat devoid of character. 'Sterile' was the word that came to Brad. Sitting in a corner of the white lobby was a white desk and behind it, a white woman in a white smock.

"Hello sir, how may I help you?"

"I would like to see Dr. Gupta please." Brad wasn't sure, but he had a sinking feeling this was the same woman he had talked to the day before.

"Do you have an appointment?"

He was almost certain now, "No, I don't, I would just like a couple of minutes of the doctor's time to ask some questions if I might."

"The doctor only takes scheduled appointments. Are you a reporter?"

Yep, this is the same one, "No, I'm a, a, just a guy interested in his research and would like to talk to him for a few minutes. That's all."

"I'm sorry Dr. Gupta is not available. Perhaps you could write a letter and one of his colleagues would be more than happy to answer your questions."

"I'm not going to write a damn letter," his voice rising. "I just want to ask the doctor a couple of questions."

"You don't have to yell and you certainly don't have to swear. As I say, sir, it is out of the…"

"I know, I heard you, I heard you yesterday. I just want a couple of minutes of his time. I just want to ask him a couple of questions. I've flown in from Detroit and all I want to do is ask him a couple of damn questions. Is it too much to ask for a few minutes of his precious time?"

"Sir, you do not have to shout. If you do not calm down, I will have to call security."

"I am calm, dammit, I'm Brad Dickson, and I can't believe you don't know who I am. I'm a superstar baseball player and I just want to ask the doctor a couple of things, that's all. Could you just tell him Brad Dickson, the baseball player, is here and wants a couple minutes of his time. Can you just do that one thing for me, huh?"

"Wait just a moment." She rose from her chair and disappeared around a corner.

She was replaced by a huge man with a crew-cut haircut, massive arms, and a pretty good-sized gun hanging off his waist.

"What can I do for you buddy," he barked as he approached the shorter Brad.

"I just want a couple of minutes of Dr. Gupta's time to ask him a few questions."

"Well, that's not gonna happen so you might want to move along, before I move you along", as he closed the distance further.

"Can you at least tell the doctor Brad Dickson would like a few minutes of his time, can you do that for me?"

"Hey, you're Brad Dickson with the Tigers? Why didn't you say so?"

Brad's spirits rose a little, "that's what I told the girl but she wasn't going to help."

"Mr. Dickson, Dr. Gupta doesn't talk to nobody he doesn't know. But I'll tell you what, let me go talk to Dr. Childress, one of the staff researchers and see if maybe he will give you some time. Sound good?"

"Sure. Anything. Thanks, uh, didn't get your name?"

"Rogers, Mr. Dickson, I'm a Sox fan, but beings the Tigers are in the Central, I'll see what I can do."

"Call me Brad. Thanks, Rogers, I really appreciate it."

Rogers disappeared and the receptionist reappeared, gave Brad the snake-eye, sat down and turned in her chair away from Brad.

"Hi there. Missed you," Brad mused. Strangely, she did not reply.

After a few minutes, Rogers returned, motioned to Brad and said, "Come with me, Mr. Dickson."

As Brad passed the receptionist, he smacked his lips as if blowing her a kiss. She still ignored him.

The two men walked down a long hallway, lined with closed doors. On the walls were alternating pictures of small animals and what looked to Brad to be pictures taken under microscopes. Each picture was framed in a wooden frame with a plaque on the bottom. Brad tried to read them as he walked by. One, a picture of a mouse read: "Toto, Left Femur 2019". Another, under what appeared to be a reddish uniformly patterned group of cells, the caption read, "Musclebot Series Six, 2023".

Toward the end of the hallway, Rogers opened a door labeled "Nano Lab #2". Inside, there was an outer office area with a simple, cleared desk and pictures hanging on the walls, similar to the ones in the hallway, and a chair.

"Wait here, Dr. Childress will be with you in a minute."

"Thanks, man."

Rogers turned and left the room, shutting the door behind him.

Brad thought he detected the smell of antiseptic. Being an athlete, he had smelled plenty of medical offices in his years. How many, he'd lost count. If he wasn't being treated for an injury, he was undergoing some test of one form or another as required on his contract or by Major League Baseball. He had spent many, many days in similar smelling offices.

After a few minutes a door at the rear of the room opened.

"Hello, Mr. Dickson, I am Dr. Childress, would you please come to my office," offering his hand to Brad. It was a strong handshake, something Brad liked. Nothing judges a man quicker than his grip in a handshake. Brad followed him into another office and sat in the chair Dr. Childress offered.

"I understand you gave Penny a hard time, both on the phone yesterday and again here today, what is it we can do for you, Mr. Dickson?"

"I'm really sorry about getting angry with her. I don't usually treat people in that manner. Please tell her I am sorry, but I have an urgent need to talk to you folks. I read on the Internet about work you do on cells and tissues."

"What do you mean by 'work we do'? We do research on the regenerative processes of living cells."

"I read where you have been able to rebuild cells, even organs."

"Yes, we have made many advances in the field of nanobiotechnology. Our goal at the Institute is to find ways to help the living organ recreate, regenerate itself."

"And you also have had recent advances involving muscles, cartilage?"

"We are in the early stages of developing ways to assist the body to rebuild these cell types, yes. But unfortunately, these cells are much more complex and unraveling nature's riddles regarding these types of cells are formidable. We are years away from being able to do this."

Brad's enthusiasm faded a bit hearing this, but pressed on.

"But you are actively researching the ability to regenerate these types of cells, like muscle tissue?"

"Mr. Dickson, it's not just a matter of saying, let's make a muscle, and put some chemicals in a test tube, heat them up and presto, muscle. We must first decode the DNA and identify the strands, or code if you will, associated with the generation of a particular type of cell. If it is muscle, we must find the part of the DNA code that makes it, and then we must isolate the code. Next we create a machine, a miniature robot, we inject with the programming to use the raw materials available and create the cells it been designed to create, just like the body does; taking the amino acids, in the right combination to create the new cells. It takes many, many tests and months of trial and error to get to that point. That's the easy part. After we think we've isolated the code, we need to find a way to reproduce it. When we are lucky, we hit upon the correct code and the correct building sequence and are then able to make the type of cell we are trying to create. The whole process could take a team literally years, if they have any success at all. So when you hear we've made a breakthrough, believe me, it was a large effort at

32

great expense. What is your interest in our work with muscle tissue?"

"Well, Doc, here's exactly how it is," now or never Brad thought. "I've bummed up my quad, and I need it fixed now. I am involved in a pennant race and have to get back in playing shape before the playoffs start in two weeks. The team's orthopedic specialist says it can't be ready in less than 6 months, probably longer, due to my age. I can't wait 6 months, I can't wait 6 weeks. I need to be ready in time for the playoffs."

"Young man, I am very sorry you have injured yourself, I really am, but we do not have a way to fix your leg, not in two weeks, maybe not in two years. The work we are doing now involves laboratory animals. If we're lucky, really lucky, we may be able to do what you suggest on a monkey in the foreseeable future, but human application is perhaps a decade away, if then. I'm sorry you've come all the way out here, but I'm afraid we cannot help you."

Childress stood up to end the conversation.

Desperately, Brad implored, "Doctor Childress, I will pay, I have a lot of money, I must get my leg fixed, I must be ready to play in two weeks."

"Son, it would take a large amount of money to fund the research needed to develop a bot capable of repairing and rebuilding a large leg muscle. Even so, the type of robot with the ability to do so is years away, even if we knew how to do it. I'm afraid your trip has been in vain."

"I have 10 million dollars."

Chapter 6

Dr. Gupta's outer office was much different than the outer office of Dr. Childress' research department. It was also sparely furnished, but the entire floor was covered with a large Indian rug. The border was made up of intricate geometric patterns woven together in red and deep brown threads. The central part of the rug featured an oval of roses surrounded by leaves with a background of orange. In one corner of the room was a cherrywood end table with brass ornaments. The legs were octagonal halfway up and joined a circular pattern and attached to the table with thick square blocks carved with floral designs. On the table sat a simple round pitcher planted with a single Song of India, lush with green, lime, and yellow leaves. The chair next to it featured a silk burgundy pad. The poles providing the back and bottom supports were white with diamond-shaped gold patterns with golden dots in the middle. The end of each pole was covered with a wide golden band. On the wall across from the table and chair was a wall length waterfall. The water cascaded gently over turquoise colored flat rock with enough jaggedness to cause the water to make a soft trickling sound. But for a door on the rear wall, this was the entire furnishings of the waiting room.

Brad had been waiting for nearly an hour, when the door opened and a young woman of Indian decent opened the door and walked to him.

"Dr. Gupta will see you now. Please follow me."

They walked through to a hallway, with a work station to one side and a closed door on the other. She gave the door a gentle knock, quietly opened it and tilted her head into the room.

"Dr. Gupta?"

"Yes, yes, show him in," Dr. Gupta instructed with a certain lack of Indian accent, "I have not much time."

Brad followed the woman into the room and immediately noticed yet another room similar in its sparse furnishing to the outer room he had just come from. A chair here, a low table there, and little else in this room as well, expect for a dozen paintings hanging on the walls which looked to be very valuable. The doctor was seated behind a heavy oak desk, upon which lay a plate glass top, reading lamp, and a small stack of manila folders. In front of the desk was a single chair, made of cane.

Brad walked up to the desk, stuck his hand out and said in his best diplomatic voice, "Dr. Gupta, Brad Dickson."

Accepting the handshake, Dr. Gupta said nothing and motioned for Brad to sit in the simple chair.

"My staff research director, Dr. Childress, tells me you are a man on a mission. A man on a mission in a hurry. A man on a mission in a hurry, with a large amount of money at his disposal. Tell me, Mr. Dickson, what makes you a man of such circumstance?"

Brad paused while the young woman exited the room, shutting the door noiselessly behind her, "Doctor, I need a miracle."

"A miracle? We are a research facility, we do not perform miracles. We devote years of research to find ways to make the human condition better. If you are looking for miracles, perhaps you should speak to a man of the cloth."

"What I need is the miracle to be able to play in the playoffs."

"Playoffs, playoffs of what?"

"Uh, well, baseball, of course". Do these people around here live in caves? "I'm the reigning MVP third baseman for the Detroit Tigers."

"Ah, yes, I have heard of them... and you," Dr. Gupta replied, nonplussed. "What is this miracle you need?"

"The day before yesterday, a base runner slid into me and tore the quad in my left leg. An MRI confirmed it. My team's doctor says I'm through and need surgery now. But I can't go that route. I have to play in the playoffs, doc, I'm 37 years old, and not getting any younger. This might be my last chance, my last chance to build on my legacy."

"But if your doctor says you need surgery, why would you not listen to him? Why would you insist on playing? Do you have so much more to prove? Do you wish for your leg to heal properly? Do you wish to be able to walk long after you are done playing baseball?" The doctor stared at Brad, waiting for the answers.

Brad hesitated, knowing Dr. Gupta truly did not understand the stakes. "Doctor, the only thing in my life is baseball. It's all I've ever known, it's the only thing I've ever been good at. And I'm very good. And besides, I'm a free agent at the end of the season. If I'm injured no one will pick me up, not at my age. But if I can produce this year, then perhaps I can play longer and add to my career numbers."

"But what is it you want me to do with your leg?"

"I want you to fix it with your nanobots."

"Ha ha, fix it with the nanobots, you say? What do you know about my nanotechnology research, Mr. Dickson?"

"I know you have created bones, and some organs. I know you are working on more complex tissues of the body. I know you recently applied for a patent concerning muscle tissue repair."

"Very good, I see you have done some homework. But Mr. Dickson, all of these things you speak of have been done with simple laboratory animals, mice and rats. We have barely scratched the surface of learning what we need to know to be able to consistently produce these cells. We are years away from applying what we have learned to humans. Mr. Dickson, nature is very complex. There are many things we have yet to learn about even our simple lab animals, let alone the human genome. I'm afraid you will find no miracle here."

"But, you are doing work with muscle, correct?"

"That is beside the point. Even if we were, what do you propose we could do for you?"

"You could inject me with those bots and repair my quad muscle in time for the playoffs."

A smile slowly formed on Dr. Gupta's face, "You think I am a mad scientist? You think I can heat up a test tube and create nanobots to repair your injury? I'm afraid I cannot."

"But you are doing research on generating muscle tissue, are you not?"

"Yes, yes we are, but it's a very complicated, slow and costly process."

"And have you successfully repaired muscle tissue?"

"Mr. Dickson I am not at liberty to discuss with you where we are with our muscle tissue research. I will tell you we know more than we did a year ago, and that is all."

"Then you ARE working on it?"

"We have made advances, yes. I can tell you we have some promising results and are pursuing some hopeful avenues. But, I must insist, we cannot help you, not now."

"Doc, all I want is the chance to be healed. All I want is the ability to play this postseason. All I want is to be able to walk out onto the field and give a show, what Brad Dickson has always given. That's all I'm asking."

Brad stood up and grimaced, limped around the chair, put his hands on the desk, leaned forward and spoke softly to the doctor, "I will do whatever it takes….whatever."

He leaned back and sat down in the chair.

Dr. Gupta rose from the desk and turned toward the window, staring out at the courtyard. Trees red with fall leaves that would someday soon litter the ground beneath. Winter would follow, laying the land stark and barren. Bone-chilling cold, wet days, dirty snow piled high on street curbs and parking lots. This once beautiful courtyard before him, soon to be devoid of activity. Only bare-limbed trees, a couple of snow-covered iron-mesh picnic tables, all waiting for the renewal of spring. He slowly turned back to Brad, who had been looking intently at the back of the doctor.

At last, he softly spoke, "Mr. Dickson, I make you no promises."

Chapter 7

Brad was taken to an examination room, where he was asked to strip to his underwear. The attending nurse told him to be seated on the table and someone would be in to take his vitals and a blood sample.

He carefully pulled off his pants and noticed that his leg, above the knee, had swollen quite a bit more since the morning. He guessed it was due to the flight and all the walking he'd done. The outer region of the swollen area was already turning a pale yellow and slowly fading into a bluish-purple toward the underside of the knee. He hopped on the table and flexed his leg. He winced as the pain shot up and down his leg. Brad lowered his left leg slowly and nearly did not have the strength to keep it from flopping back against the table. He slipped his arms through the openings in the gown and waited.

A nurse entered the room. She carried a small tray with tubes, blood pressure cuff, gauze packs and tape. She asked for his arm, wrapped a rubber band around his bicep and asked him to squeeze his fist. After she was done drawing the blood, she took his blood pressure and pulse. Brad tried to make eye contact with her, but she concentrated on her task and did not look up at him. She finished her work, loaded up her tray and was gone.

A few minutes passed and another nurse entered the room. She had a tool Brad recognized as a reflex tester. She took his good right leg under the knee, and lightly tapped the hammer on the base of the knee. The leg reflexively shot out a few inches. She took his bad left leg next, slowly putting her hand behind the knee, watching Brad's face and slowed as his face showed an obvious grimace. "Sorry, sir, I need to evaluate the reflexivity of your injured leg."

"I know, just please be careful, it's awfully sore."

She gently tapped the knee, sending ice picks of pain up brad's leg. He cried out at the suddenness of the agony.

"I'm so sorry, but you can relax, I'm done now." With that she gathered her tools and left.

The attending nurse reentered the room and told Brad, "You can put your clothes back on. When you are ready just come out into the hall, I'll be waiting for you."

As he dressed he tried to count the times he'd been in an examination room over the years.

Too many times to count.

Every year before the season, for contractual purposes, he would go through a battery of tests to determine his physical status. Every inch of his body was tested. He did stress tests, blood tests, brain tests, and tests to determine his body fat. Endurance tests to see how much air would fit in his lungs. Tests of agility, tests of endurance, tests to determine if his hand/eye coordination was the same as it had been the previous spring. Then, during the season, more tests. The scheduled monthly tests of checking the physical wear and tear, drug tests, tests when he tweaked a muscle, or got hit by a pitch. There was nothing the medical staff of the Detroit Tigers did not know about his body.

He stepped into the hall. The nurse motioned for him to follow her. They ended up back in the outer office of Dr. Gupta. Brad sat again in the cushioned chair and waited.

Chapter 8

Dr. Gupta had walked to the primary research laboratory of Nano Robotics after talking with Brad. He had in fact made a recent breakthrough in synthesizing the amino acid combination in rebuilding dystrophic muscle on a mouse. He walked over to the mouse's cage and watched it spin the wheel at a slow pace. Not bad, he thought, considering this little guy had his leg muscle completely removed a week ago. The mouse's shaved leg showed the smallest hint of a muscle forming around the hip joint. The bright red stringy tissue looked healthy and uninfected. He grabbed a food pellet and offered it to the mouse who stopped the wheel, looked at the food, grabbed it with its front legs and began gnawing on it. When finished, it hopped back on the wheel and started walking once more.

If only it were that simple, thought Dr. Rasheesh Gupta as he turned and left the room, heading back to his office.

When Brad was escorted back to Dr. Gupta's office, he sat again in the cane chair and waited as the doctor was thumbing through a stack of papers in a folder.

"Well, Brad, it appears you are in good health," he said looking up over the folder at Brad.

"Your tests have all come back normal. We are still waiting on the results of some DNA sequencing tests that take a little longer to process, but I think we can move forward. What you are asking me to do, to fix your quadriceps muscle, entails a very complex situation that requires an equally complex solution. We must first identify the amino acid levels and composition within your body – precisely. Any error and the coding will not work. When we have produced a map of your body's chemistry makeup, we then match that against the genes we know make up the processes to create muscle tissue. Fortunately, the human body genome was decoded back at the turn of the century, and through further definition and research, we have identified the genes in the sequence responsible for cell production. What we do at the Institute is to create chemical agents, machines, which are given instructions to build cells. It is really quite simple in execution. Think of the beginning of the Iron Age. Centuries ago, man looked around and saw shiny particles in the earth around him. He sifted that earth until he accumulated a good supply of the shiny elements. He hit upon the idea of heating this shiny dirt and it was separated from the other earth by the heat. Enough of it and he started thinking of ways to use it. Great factories eventually were built to produce tools, machines, everything man could imagine to help make his life easier and more productive. Our molecular factory is no different. The nanobots are given instructions, chemically, to mimic the natural building processes of life. To take the raw materials, in this case, amino acids, and set up a factory to manufacture cells they have been programmed to create. We started with skin, the simplest of cells. We told a nanobot to attach itself to the skinned leg of a mouse. With the instructions the nanobot was given, it produced skin. It reskinned the mouse's entire leg. That process took nearly two months. We have continuously progressed to create more and more complex cells. And at the same time, creating many bots to do the work, which has reduced the time it takes to set up the factory and go into production. We can now reskin the leg of a mouse in 24 hours.

But we are talking about a much more complex cell and process when we look at a muscle cell. A muscle cell, or myocyte, is a long, tubular cell that arises developmentally from myoblasts to form muscles. There are various specialized forms of myocytes: cardiac, skeletal, and smooth muscle cells, with various properties. Cardiac myocytes, for instance, are responsible for generating the electrical impulses that control the heart rate, among other things. Each myocyte contains myofibrils, which are very long chains of sarcomeres, the contractile units of the cell. A cell from the bicep's brachii muscle, for instance, may contain 100,000 sarcomeres. The myofibrils of smooth muscle cells are not arranged into sarcomeres. The sarcomeres are composed of thin and thick filaments. Thin filaments are actin filaments, whereas thick filaments consist of an arrangement of myosin proteins. The sarcomere does not contain organelles or a nucleus. Individual muscle fibrils are surrounded by endomysium." Dr. Gupta paused to fill a glass with water, took a drink and continued, "Within the muscle cell, the myofibrils are bound together by perimysium and formed into bundles called fascicles; the bundles are then grouped together to form muscle tissue, which is enclosed in a sheath of epimysium. Muscle spindles are distributed throughout the muscles and provide sensory feedback information to the central nervous system.

A myoblast is a type of embryonic progenitor cell that differentiates to give rise to muscle cells. Skeletal muscle fibers are made when myoblasts fuse together; muscle fibers therefore have

46

multiple nuclei, each nucleus originating from a single myoblast. The fusion of myoblasts is specific to skeletal muscle and not cardiac muscle or smooth muscle.

Myoblasts that do not form muscle fibers dedifferentiate back into satellite cells. These satellite cells remain adjacent to a muscle fiber, situated between the sarcolemma and the endomysium.

As you can see, this is a very complex process. We must create a nanobot capable of mimicking all of these steps in order to form a muscle. Any wrong instruction, or wrong sequence, will make the factory totally useless at best and produce something unintended at worst. The trick is to make sure we code the nanobots to mine and convert the proper chemicals at the proper time. It is this aspect of nanobiotechnology where we here at Nano Robotics have a distinct advantage. We have discovered the language of nature.

Everything in the natural world occurs in relation to time. Chemical reactions have a distinct half life. When the proper mixture of chemicals has been reacting for the proper amount of time, the result is what had been intended. Take for instance the formation of an embryo. At specific time intervals, various functions are fired which cause the formation of the various cells of the developing organism. When it's time for the stomach to begin forming, a signal is sent and the proper chemicals are mined and they are fused in a sort of baking process. At the proper time, the baking is stopped and the resulting mass is the beginning of the stomach. We know this to be true because in our research, we have intentionally stopped the process right after it began, and the creation of the organ, the stomach in this case, is muted. Until recently, we did not know how to turn this switch back on but we have now developed the means to communicate with the factory. After we've stopped the process, we can send commands via chemical combinations to tell the factory to start up production again and continue the stomach building. We've been able to stop the process and restart as many as 5 times with varying delay timers."

Brad tried hard to comprehend, but he was obviously very lost.

The doctor continued, "The next challenge was then to figure out how to start the process on our own without the help of the natural processes. This took many long hours and hundreds, if not thousands of failed tests before we started to find success with it. Again, we started slowly with the most primitive of living cells, the skin. We discovered the exact timings and chemicals needed to create the first skin cells to develop within the embryonic stage. After that, it was simply a matter of trial and error to determine the optimum time to inject the chemical 'instructions' into the DNA's factory.

Later, when we started tackling more complex cells, the task grew more daunting and riskier. We would get the process started, but the cells would become malformed. We could not figure out why until we hit on the idea that the makeup of the development process changes as a function of time. In other words, at the beginning of developing complex cells, the process is mainly concerned with just creating living mass, but after the initial stages, the specialization of the various cells of the organ or body component has to be kick started. We had not factored in time as a vital component of the process. Once we realized this, we made great strides. We now can create most of the vital organs of mice

48

as well as some of the specialized cellular structures, such as cartilage and muscle."

"Doctor Gupta, that's exactly what I'm looking for!"

"But of course you are, Mr. Dickson. We are talking about mice here, primitive creatures that are not only smaller than humans, but much less complex. Even though a mouse's DNA is roughly 97.5% that of matching human DNA, that 2.5% represents the most complex cell production functions. More complex organ functionality, expanded bone growth, everything needed to produce a larger animal, and all things growing at the same rate as to not make any one organ or limb, or blood vessel disproportionately large or small. At the top literally, is the complexity involved in development of the human brain tissue. In the 100 million years since man and mouse had shared a common ancestor, the human DNA has evolved at what may appear to be a slow pace, but none the less the change, as we know, is dramatic. I cannot just take the language that we have decoded for a mouse and fix your leg.

"How complex is the coding for muscle tissue," Brad asked, wanting the doctor to focus on his particular need, "that is, how much different is a mouse's leg muscle than mine?"

Dr. Gupta lifted Brad's MRI off of his desk and studied it for a few moments before answering, "Mr. Dickson, there is a group of muscles that together form the bond between the hip and the knee. The group is called the quadriceps femoris, or taking the literal Latin for "four-headed muscle of the femur", also called simply the quadriceps. The quadriceps extensor, or quads, is a large muscle group that includes the four muscles on the front of the thigh. It is

49

the great extensor muscle of the knee, forming a large fleshy mass which covers the front and sides of the femur. You have managed to damage the largest of the four, the vastus lateralis, or the'lateral' side of the femur, In other words, your outer thigh muscle. Being the largest, it has the most complex building code of the four. A mouse does not stand upright, so its leg muscles have evolved in different way. There are only two muscles connecting a mouse's hip to its knee. In the earlier part of the century, there was promising research involving injection of stem cells into damaged muscles in mice. The healing time was greatly reduced. But stem cell research fell out of favor when the government stopped funding stem cell research facilities. Ours is the only research that I know of that has been able to exceed the success rate of the stem cell researchers."

"And you can use what you've learned with mice on me?"

"We just do not have the data needed to code the process properly. We are pretty sure we know what steps to take and what programming is needed to build the vastus lateralis, but we are many months, if not years, away from attempting it on a human subject."

"As you are well aware, I am here to help you to jumpstart your research."

"Yes, I am. As you are aware, you are taking a great risk."

"But, you will be able to shortcut years of research."

"There is a very great chance this will be a failed experiment. We just do not know precisely what the timing of the human vastus lateralis chemical and material build is."

"What's the worst case if it fails? You are not able to build my leg back up, and I miss the post season? But if you are successful, you will have lopped off years of research time and effort and proven to the world your methods can work on humans. For me, what it means is I'm able to make it to the playoffs and extend my career. That is the most important thing to me."

"I remind you, it is highly likely that it will fail."

"In that case, you will learn what not to do next time."

"You could have permanent leg damage, you might never play again."

"That's a risk I'm willing to take, doc."

"You have to leave me completely guiltless if this does not work."

"I will sign a contract to that effect if that's what you want. I'll sign anything you want. I'll sign it right now. You could win the MVP for science, if they have such a thing."

Dr. Gupta was already thinking the Nobel Prize for medicine would certainly be an appropriate reward for such an achievement. "OK, Mr. Dickson, I will help you, but you must be aware, I cannot guarantee you anything."

"I am only asking you to try".

"You could end up worse off than you are now".

"Doc, what could be worse than missing the playoffs?"

Chapter 9

Over the course of the next two days, Brad was put through a grueling series of tests and medical procedures. A seemingly endless series of blood drawings and other bodily fluids were taken every two hours. At rest and at work stress tests in addition to anechoic chamber tests. Tests were given before and after each meal, before and after every activity for that matter.

"We need to get a precise template of your body's chemical production", one of the nurses tried to explain.

It was an exhausting two days and Brad wondered if he would survive the testing long enough to get to the cure.

On the morning of the third day, Brad met with Dr. Gupta. The doctor had a thick folder of Brad's test results and was thumbing through the pages as Brad entered his office.

"I believe we are ready, Mr. Dickson."

"I know I am", Brad confidently shot back.

"I have not explained the exact process to you yet, because frankly, I did not know what the exact process would be. But we now have a roadmap and are ready to proceed."

Brad sat down in the simple cane chair as Dr. Gupta continued.

"This process as I explained before requires the seeding of living tissue to coalesce into a mass. We will first inject your knee with a concoction of fluid that occurs naturally in the body. But because we are concentrating on a specific production process, we will only include those fluids and chemicals that are instrumental in the

52

creation of muscle tissue. Since you already have muscle tissue, we will not attempt to make a muscle; rather we have developed a plan where the factory we create is more like a repair shop on steroids. Our fluid will be injected into your existing vastus lateralis with tiny chemical machines included that you know as nanobots. These molecular machines are the workmen to build up the cells of your muscle. It is a process we call molecular assembler. They receive the messenger RNA instructions and go to work. We have determined an exact number of nanobots needed to do the repair. Any less and the job would not get finished, any more and the muscle would become abnormally large. There are three types of nanobots that will be created and injected into your body. For clarity, I will use laymen terms to describe the process to you so you will understand. The first type is the miner bots. These machines will collect the additional raw materials needed to build the muscle tissue. They will continuously journey through your body looking for and bringing back to the construction site the fluids, acids, and proteins needed for the building process. They make up roughly 88% of the nanobots infused into your body. The second type of nanobots will be the builder bots. This group will be responsible for taking the raw materials and imitating what the body naturally does to regenerate tissue. They will initiate the process to mix the ingredients brought by the miner bots and begin by creating the muscle stem cells needed to turn the cells into muscle tissue. These nanobots make up nearly 12 % of the total given to you. The third type of nanobots is the director bots. Their job as you might guess is to make sure the other groups are working together and functioning properly. They constantly monitor the production, ensuring the miner bots are getting enough

53

raw materials to the building site and the builders are mixing and assembling the ingredient properly at the proper rate. Throughout the process, the director bots monitor the changing workload and place miners and builders where they are needed. When the building is completed, the directors guide all the bots to the kidney, where they are dispelled from the body in urine. The process is similar to that of a bee hive at work, or the building of an ant hill, but on a much smaller scale. Each builder bot is instructed to adhere itself to your muscle tissue and hyper propagate. It's a term we use to mean rapid growth. At the point where the muscle is completely reformed, the process will stop and the remaining fluid will be absorbed into your body. While the hyper propagation is taking place, the newly created cells will replace damaged ones, adhere themselves to healthy ones and reform the strong bonds which are so important to muscle tissue. If all goes well, based on our best guess, this process should take between seven and ten days. During this time we will provide round the clock observation to ensure all is going as hoped. We must control your activities, your food intake, even the air you breathe, in order to create the ideal construction site."

"The unions will be proud," Brad mused.

Dr. Gupta, ignoring the crude reference continued, "For your part, you must do the things we ask of you without fail. You must properly teach the muscle how to behave as it is being rebuilt. We will have an intensive physical therapy regimen for you to follow. We will build the muscle, but you must teach it to behave properly. In a few minutes, the nurse will come for you and take you to the surgical center, where you will be prepared for the injection. Do you have any questions at this time Mr. Dickson?"

"Doc, this has all happened pretty fast. Even so, the more I'm around you and your team; the more confident I get this is going to work. A few days ago, there was not a chance in hell I'd be able to play in the playoffs but now, now I see myself getting back in the lineup and continuing my career. Even if this doesn't work, I just want you to know that I thank you for all you've done for me and all you are going to do for me."

Dr. Gupta smiled, but didn't respond. He was already thinking how he would put that $10 million to good use.

Brad lay on the gurney, wrapped in a thin gown, which barely covered his six and a half foot frame. A slight breeze in the room made it a little cool and uncomfortable. The nurse had been gone a long time. Let's get on with it, Brad thought. From his perspective on the gurney, he could only see forward and to the sides, but not behind him. The room was brightly lit and contained a number of machines, one of which was connected to the line going into his arm. He could hear a monotonous beep, which he realized was the sound of his own heart. Nice and steady and slow.

A man entered his peripheral vision but he couldn't make out who it was due to the full mask he wore. "How are you doing Brad?" The familiar voice belonged to one of the doctors that had been putting him through the testing these past couple of days.

"Pretty good, I'm ready."

"We are just about ready too. We just need to get everyone in here and wait for you to say bye bye."

Brad barely heard the words as the drugs delivered through the line attached to his arm began to take effect. He was at third base on the little league field in his hometown by the time the doctor's sentence ended.

Dr. Gupta entered the room and addressed the team, "Ladies and gentlemen we are about to perform an historical procedure. The future of nanobiotics will be greatly advanced today, thanks to the dedication and hard work of each and every one of you. You will be able to tell your children you were there when the very first step of human immortality was taken. What we do here today will allow mankind to live virtually forever. Someday, mankind will never need to worry about parts wearing out, mending broken bones, succumbing to the ravages of aging. We are about to show the world than the human body can be repaired in every way and someday soon we will need not worry about death, but live our lives to the fullest, not worrying about disease, nor fearing the inevitable end. We will be able to live many lifetimes, as mankind has always dreamt. Not constrained by what we hope to accomplish in one lifetime, because we will be able to experience many. No more disease, no more deformities, no more mental illness, no more birth defects. All of these things will be preventable and curable. Let's begin the new chapter in human evolution, the chapter where we take direct control of the outcome."

With that, he walked to Brad's side, called for the syringe that contained the nanobots, leaned over Brad's leg and pushed the needle deep into his thigh.

Chapter 10

The Tigers were in the field. It was a beautiful sunny afternoon in Detroit. Brad was floating, hovering, above the stadium. He thought it funny they were playing a day game and he was not in the lineup. He was always in the lineup. He was always playing or thinking about playing baseball........

For as long as he could remember, he had been interested in baseball and only baseball. His dad had taught him to catch and throw when he was barely three years old. His whole day revolved around the game. After school he would grab his mitt and play burny-out, or catch-a-fly-your-up or pickle with his buddies until dark. Most nights, after supper and homework, he would tune in Sirius and listen to his favorite team, the Braves. He would often drift off to sleep and miss the end, especially when they were on a west coast swing. It was a very special day when he would actually get to see his team when they were in town playing the local Phillies. Brad had been raised a Phillies fan. Everyone he knew was a Phillies fan, including his dad and uncles, but when Zach Faraday, a slugger for the Braves, hit a grand slam in the 10th inning against the home town boys, Brad's allegiance was forever transferred when the ball landed in his glove. At the time, he was heartbroken that Zach had beaten the Phillies, but the more he looked at that ball on his dresser, the more he became attached to Zach, and finally the whole team. His friends kidded him and made fun of him, but he remained loyal to Zach and the Braves.

As Brad got older, his natural talent became clear. Real clear. He stuck out like a sore thumb when playing with the other guys in the neighborhood. His dad signed him up when he was 10 for a traveling all-star team made up of the local elite players his age. It didn't take long for him to become the star of those all-star teams. They beat everyone they played. Brad was tall for his age and easily could hit the ball over the fences of the little league parks they played in. Every position they played him, he excelled. Many times he would pitch a no hitter and have three home runs in the same game. He was a natural. He had all the skills the game required, strong throwing arm, power hitter, speed on the bases, and quickness in the field. He had it all. As he entered his teens, he was asked to join a team made up of the top players from the entire state of Pennsylvania. His team played teams made up of other states' stars. He often won MVP honors at these tournaments. He made it look easy as he stroked a home run or struck out another batter. While still in his early teens, he received calls from major league scouts and college coaches. He listened to scouts as they told him how much money he could make, and how much their club would pay, just to have him sign. The college coaches would sit in their living room and argue Brad needed to get an education just in case professional baseball was not in his future. In those days, there was a lot of pressure on him to take the money, as his family was not well off and he knew they had spent a fortune over the years on his baseball activities. In the end, his father convinced him he needed to go to college and get an education. So he enrolled at Texas, was named to a couple All-American teams and led the Longhorns to the College World series three times, finally winning in his senior year.

It was a foregone conclusion he would be the number one pick in the following year's draft. The lowly Washington Nationals, having had the distinction of losing 102 games in 2008, became the lucky franchise with the first pick, and of course, they chose him. Detroit, coming off a down year themselves, finishing in the basement of the American League Central, and in need of power hitting, finally convinced Washington to trade the top prospect for 6 players, 2 draft picks and $5 million cash. He spent a short amount of time in Erie, with the AA SeaWolves, but was promoted to the big club toward the end of July, and helped the Tigers turn around somewhat with an 86-77 record and hit .312 for the 70 games he played. The next year was his big breakthrough year where he achieved what everyone had expected, .341 average, 37 homers and 131 RBIs, all records for a rookie, and he was rewarded with the 2010 MVP award as well as the Rookie of the Year, becoming only the third player in major league baseball history, with Fred Lynn and Ichiro Suzuki, to receive both honors in the same year.

Things just got better. Each year brought improved stats, and increases in pay. The Tigers had made it to the playoffs every year since; winning the World Series 4 times along the way. But beginning in '21, he started noticing the aches in his body were becoming worse and more frequent. Initially it was just soreness at the start of spring training which was not particularly worrisome, since he had slowed down in his off-season training regimen. He expected it to hurt a little getting himself into playing shape, and it did. A couple of weeks in and he was as strong as ever. However, a late season ankle injury slowed him down and by not playing every day, he was not as sharp and effective at the end of the season as he would have liked. Partially due to his condition, the Tigers were quickly dispatched by the Twins that year.

He grew even less committed to off-season training while nursing the ankle back to full health in 2022, and it showed. The Tigers, and Brad seemed to have peaked.

However, in 2023, he brought a renewed desire and he came to camp in great shape for a 35 year old. But another injury, this time his throwing arm, slowed him down and caused him a great deal of pain during the summer. His team lost in the first round again, but he had a good series to top off a year where he led the American League in homers with 47. His batting average did however decline a bit, and although he would not have admitted it openly, he sensed his swing had slowed a little and detected an ever so slight delay when pulling the trigger.

He maintained a strong training schedule that winter and played the '24 season injury free, for the first time in two years, hitting 52 homers and batting .312.

Not so with the current season. He injured his ankle again in a freak spring training collision and started the season on the DL. It took him until mid-May to get into playing shape and nearly the all-star break before he felt 100 %. Then he injured the other ankle and played through July in a great deal of pain. His numbers reflected his physical problems. But he played through. He was seeing and hitting the ball again as the Tigers came down the stretch in September. Then just as they were making a final push, with a 7 game winning streak, the jerk Rodriquez made a hard slide, one that was unneeded and clearly illegal, that had torn his vastus lateralis.

He looked down again into the stadium, and the field and stands were empty. The lights were on and it was getting dark. Then the stadium faded and finally disappeared below him.

Chapter 11

Brad's eyes popped open. The bright, stark room light was painful, and he squinted. The IV drip pole and bag came into focus first, then the television, then the chalkboard. He could only make out one name on the board, Susie, the on duty RN. He looked to the right out the window and saw a three-story brick building with few windows. The television was tuned to ESPN, Brad's favorite channel. He reckoned the staff had assumed he would want to watch sports. They assumed correctly. The sound was turned off but Brad could tell the story being played was about the weekend's NFL football games. He wasn't particularly interested in football, but included those pro jocks into his 'club'. It appeared the Bears had beaten the Packers again. So what? He looked back over to the IV drip. The bag was opaque and the liquid clear. On the bag he could read "Cefazolin". Brad thought it must be some kind of pain medicine, since at the moment, he felt no pain. In fact he felt better than he could remember feeling for many years.

He grabbed the bed railing with his left hand and pulled himself toward the edge. He gingerly tried to lift his left leg, and a hot iron shot of pain immediately stopped him. He flopped back down on the bed, dejected. The process is not working. He tried a few more times and try as he might, he could not lift the leg without a great deal of pain. After a few more feeble attempts he stopped. He remembered what Dr. Gupta had told him, not to expect results immediately. How long would it take, he did not know. He only knew the time he had, two weeks.

Dr. Childress had filled Brad in on recent experimentation. The mice were responding to and starting cell growth within twelve hours of nanobot injection. He knew he needed to be patient. He grabbed for the remote and turned the volume up. The commentators were discussing the Broncos game. Brad wasn't really interested in what he was hearing; his mind was on more pressing matters, like when was he going to get out of here. He had to get ready for the playoffs, he had things to do with his life, after all, this was the first day of the rest of his life, and he didn't want to waste any of it.

A nurse entered his room.

"How are we feeling Mr. Dickson?"

"I don't know how you are feeling but my leg is killing me."

"That's to be expected," she reassured him. "It takes time for the boots to get to work."

"Don't you mean 'bots'," he quizzed.

She giggled, "The staff calls them 'boots', cuz they're like new trainees at boot camp. They're brought to the training center, given some basic instructions and within six weeks, they're full-fledged soldiers, lean, mean fighting machines."

"Six weeks? They better be special forces, because I don't have six weeks," Brad countered.

Brad pointed at the drip bag.

"Antibiotics," she responded, anticipating his question. "We don't want to lose the war in the first battle, now do we?"

The nurse took his vitals, drew some blood and was gone still musing over Brad's earlier reply.

She had been gone but a few minutes, and the door opened. It was Dr. Gupta. He looked fresh, like he had just showered and shaved.

"Good afternoon, Mr. Dickson, how are we feeling?"

"I feel pretty good doc, but I can't lift my leg, it feels as bad as it's ever felt."

"Do not worry about that Mr. Dickson; it is still just a little early for any significant progress to occur. We injected the nanobots only a short while ago."

"How long should it be before I start to feel better," Brad asked.

"As we discussed in my office yesterday, it takes time for the mending process to begin. It has only been 4 hours since the nanobots were injected into your leg. First of all, they have to settle down. The injection process is a bit traumatic, even for robots. Once they acclimate to your body's chemical makeup and temperature, they will organize and make the journey to the site of the injury. We have instructed the builders and directors to pass from the injection site and regroup at the lower end of your vastus lateralis, where the muscle has been torn. There, they will set up the work site. The miner bots meanwhile will basically make a circumnavigation of your entire body, via the blood vessels. On their journey, they will note where certain chemicals, acids and proteins can be found. We have programmed them to look in areas that will have a high concentration of the materials needed. They will gather up enough of these materials to begin the base cell construction. When 90% of the miner bots have checked in and the directors have inventoried their cargo, the directors will give the command for the builders to begin. Each director is assign to a group of builders and in turn, a group of miners are assigned to each builder. There is redundancy built into the organization in case of individual failure. In such a case, bots will be automatically reassigned. The process will continue; my bots do not take breaks, until your muscle is rebuilt. Then, the nanobots will make their way to your kidney and be discharged the next time you urinate. We have estimated the total time for the entire process to be 10 days.

During the 10 days, you will begin a rehabilitation process that will further influence the building process and you teach the new cells in your muscle how to perform. We will slowly at first work with your knee to strengthen the existing muscle. The new muscle tissue being produced will acclimate to the activity and also become strengthened as the cells are produced and brought online with your other living tissue. At the end of the 10 days, if we have succeeded, you will be back on the baseball field, good as new."

Brad looked down at his swollen, purple knee and tried to see or feel the machines at work.

"You will not be able to see what is happening," Dr. Gupta sensed Brad's quizzical stare. "But you may feel them, especially toward the end of the process. Each bot has a radioactive marker, so we can track each and every one of them. If you want to see them at work, you can with the radioscope. In a while, we will take you to the monitor room and we will be able to see what your bots are up to."

Brad thought he could feel the machines in his knee, but figured in was in his head. "Doc, what if a bot or group of bots calls in sick, you know, malfunctions in some way, or breaks, what do you do then?"

"The directors have instructions to dismantle a bot if it becomes defective. The machine is literally torn apart and the various pieces are assimilated into your body, where they eventually will be flushed out vie your normal regeneration process."

"Who directs the directors?"

"Do not worry Mr. Dickson; we have a triple backup protocol the directors follow. We have never had a director malfunction."

"But what if…"

Dr. Gupta anticipated the question, "If it came down to it, where the build was not going properly, where the miners malfunctioned and did not delivery the proper materials or the correct ratio of materials, or say the builders started constructing something other than the tissue they are programmed to build, or the directors ignored the workers or became inoperative, we always have the ability to reprogram the nanobots. If that doesn't work and all else fails, we have a 'fail safe' command which will order all nanobots to turn off and we can then extract them directly using radioactive tracers. So you see Mr. Dickson, we have thought of everything, so you need not worry."

"Who said I was worried." Brad closed his eyes, the whirlwind of activities the past few days finally taking a toll on him. Within seconds, he was asleep.

Dr. Gupta, took Brad's wrist, instinctively and subconsciously checked his pulse, smiled to himself and left the room.

Chapter 12

"Mr. Dickson how are you feeling this morning," the cheery nurse whom Brad remembered from the day before said as she plumped up his pillow. "You had a good night's sleep."

"I feel great, how are my little boots doing."

"I'm sorry, I don't know. When I'm done here, let's go down to the control room and you can take a peek."

She opened his blinds, straightened a chair, went into the hallway and brought back a tray of eggs, pancakes and bacon and a glass of orange juice. "East your breakfast and I'll take you down there when you are finished."

Brad hurriedly ate the meal. He realized he hadn't eaten since before his operation and his stomach thought his throat had been cut. When he was done, the nurse took the tray out into the hallway, came back in, lowered the rail on his bed, and helped him lift his legs over the side. She produced a wheelchair and guided him into it.

Halfway down the hall, they took a left, through a double door and then another left into a room full of monitors. It reminded Brad of an air traffic control room he had seen in a movie. There were two technicians in the room. They both looked up briefly when the pair entered the room, and just as quickly, returned to their work. One of the technicians was seated at a desk with a large monitor. The screen was filled with dots, thousands of them, red, green, and blue. Some were moving slowly around the screen, but most of them stationary. Brad realized the area the dots were enclosed in looked like a human leg, from just above the knee to just below.

Anticipating Brad's question, one of the technicians spoke up, "This is your, should we say, 'jobsite' Mr. Dickson. Where our little guys are rebuilding your leg muscle."

The blue ones up here on the move," the other technician said, pointing at an area above the knee, "are returning to the worksite, the blue ones moving up away from your knee are going to get more materials. The green and red ones concentrated around the knee area are either builders or directors."

"Please call me Brad. How many are there? It looks like thousands."

The first technician looked up, "Brad, here on my screen you can read the counts. Number of miners, builders, and directors that are actively working in this first column, and the number of bots that have malfunctioned or for some reason are not accomplishing their mission or have stopped communicating with us are in the second column.

Brad read the first column numbers:

Miners – 32146

Builders – 4317

Directors – 194

And then the second column:

Miners – 276

Builders – 47

"Why so many in the second column?" Brad asked, more than a little concerned.

"Ha, don't worry Brad; your leg is getting fixed. We always have casualties upon initial injection, the process is quiet vigorous and we expect to lose some. There is a margin of safety of .05 % and we are well within tolerance. After the initial injection settle-in phase, only a handful of your bots have gone offline. We don't expect much more loss during the course of the build."

"I hope not, I can use all the bots I can get! Dr. Gupta told me the instructions can be changed, how does that happen?"

"With this system, we can get into the programming suite and send new instructions to the nanobots. You have to be in the room over there," the first technician said, pointing his thumb to a locked door, "it's kind of like an x-ray machine. The difference is our rays are used to download instructions to the nanos."

The nurse wheeled Brad around and they were almost to the door when another station on the far side of the room caught his eye. At the station was a lockbox-looking contraption hung above a table. On the table was a smaller monitor, with a keyboard attached to it. A card on top of the monitor read 'Secured Station'.

"What's that device for," Brad asked.

The technicians looked at each other then at the nurse and back to Brad. Finally the seated one said, "That's the Waterloo computer."

"Waterloo," Brad asked, "what's that mean?"

"Dr. Childress has this thing about the military and military history. It's his idea of being funny, you know 'meet your Waterloo', like Napoleon. If anything goes wrong, we can get on that system and kill all your robots. But we've never used it, and I'm sure we will never have the need."

"That's reassuring," Brad smiled. "I suppose the lockbox is like the one used in that old time movie 'War Games'."

"I suppose," the standing technician answered, not having a clue what Brad was talking about. "The only people who have the keys are Dr. Gupta and Dr. Childress."

Satisfied, Brad looked away and the nurse wheeled him down the hall to the physical therapy room. There, the therapists worked on his leg, measuring his uplift strength then his downlift strength. They wasted no time and put him on a treadmill, where he started at a slow walk, limping noticeably. The physical therapist gradually increased to a fairly brisk walk. Brad noticed the pain in his leg seemed to be less than it had been earlier.

After ten minutes on the treadmill, one therapist asked, "How does the leg feel, Mr. Dickson?"

"Please call me Brad, what's your name honey?"

"Cheryl, Brad, Cheryl Gibson," she blushed.

"Well, Cheryl, it feels a lot better than it did a couple of days ago, even a couple of hours ago."

"That's terrific, Brad. The strength tests also confirm your leg has gotten 7% stronger than it was when you first were tested. We will have you back to 100% in no time."

"You've got 10 days," Brad said, "so you better be right."

Chapter 13

Back in his room, Brad had just finished dinner when he thought of Marisa. During these last few days, he had told her next to nothing of what was going on. He did not want to worry her, but even more, he did not want her to accidentally let anyone know where he was. He told her he was in Chicago for some tests and to visit a specialist for a second opinion. He knew she was used to him being gone for days, playing away games, talking to his agent, lining up business deals or hunting or fishing with the guys, so she probably didn't think too much about the reason and duration of this trip.

Brad felt the situation was stabilized, the operation worked, and the bots seemed to be doing their magic, so he thought there would be no harm to let her in on what was happening to him.

He picked up his cellphone and dialed her.

"Hi Baby," her sweet voice cooed into his ear. "How are the tests going? Will you be home soon?"

"The tests are going fine, Mar, I need to tell you something," and with that he proceeded to tell her all about Nano Robotics, Dr. Gupta, the company's promising research, and what they were doing to repair his leg.

After an uncomfortably long pause, she spoke, "Does Dr. Lewis know about this?"

"No. It is of no concern to him."

"Does Al Simpson know about it?"

"No, he doesn't have a clue."

"Have you talked to Bob about it?"

"No, I don't need any of them to know about this, and I certainly don't need their approval," Brad shot back, getting tired of the grilling. "I'm the only one who decides about my future. Me." Taking a couple of deep breaths to calm down a little, Brad said, "My leg is getting better already. The test I had today confirms it, 7% improvement of strength since the injection."

"Can you feel them," Marisa asked, trying to grasp this information and picture what these little gizmos looked like. She had formed a picture of tiny robots like the one in Lost in Space, scampering around inside Brad's leg.

"I don't know, I think maybe I can. I definitely feel some tingling in my quad. I don't know if it's the nanobots or just my leg healing. Either way, it feels great."

"So, when will you be home?"

"The plan is I will be here another nine days for observation and therapy. I should be home by the 29th."

"Mr. Yorkey has called a couple times asking how you are doing."

"What have you told him?"

"I just said you were having some testing done and resting your leg."

"Good, that's all I want him or anyone for that matter to know right now." Brad rubbed his forehead, "Mar, I'm kinda bushed and need to lay down. I think I'll let you go for now. OK?"

"OK, baby, love you. Get some sleep."

"Me too." Brad hung up the phone and dialed his agent.

Chapter 14

The therapy treatments were going great. Each session brought a higher strength number and the periods on the treadmill were getting longer and faster. By the fifth day, Brad's leg was feeling good. He was amazed by the flexibility in his knee, and his ability to run on the injured leg. He hadn't seen much of Dr. Childress and even less of Dr. Gupta, who would pop in once a day to ask him how he was doing. Dr. Childress was a little more involved with his daily regimen, testing the strength and flexibility of his leg each morning and evening. He was impressed with the progress that Brad was making.

Each day Brad would go to the control room and ask how his bots were doing. There had been a few more casualties, but he grew more confident in the nanobots and his investment into Nano Robotics.

"You have a visitor, Mr. Dickson. There is a gentleman waiting in the outer office," Penny called over the intercom as his treadmill session was wrapping up. Brad toweled himself off and hurried to the front office.

"Barry, my man! How ya doin?" Brad said as he entered the room and shook hands with his agent, "what's the good word?"

Barry Johnson had been Brad's agent from the beginning. Brad had been his first client under contract, and Brad's abilities had made him very rich.

"I did what you asked, I talked to Yorkey about next year."

"And?"

"And he was pretty elusive. He asked how you were doing, what your rehab plans this winter would be, when you would be ready. When I didn't have good answers for any of his questions, he got defensive and clammed up a bit. He talked about how the team will miss you if they make it to the playoffs. He talked about your numbers being off because of your DL visits this summer. He didn't really go into anything much further. I quizzed him a bit, tried to explain some of the special circumstances, told him this injury was directly the fault of another player, and that it didn't have anything to do with your age. He agreed, but kind of left the whole discussion hanging. So I finally left. It was kind of awkward."

"Come, on Barry, you've talked to him hundreds of times, give me your gut."

"My gut? My guy says he's hedging. He thinks you are past helping his club and he's thinking of ways to save money or get some fresh meat in here. My bet is he's looking to either offer you less or who knows, maybe even talk to you about authorizing a trade. I really didn't get a good read, and that bothers me. I usually can read Yorkey like a book. Hey man enough about that right now, how's your leg?"

"My leg feels fantastic. It's a frickin miracle Barry. I'm running!! Can you believe that?"

"So what did they do, give you a bionic leg? Gonna be Steve Austin, man?"

"No, none of that sci-fi bull. This is real. I don't have a bionic leg or any of that crap. There are little robots called nanobots that are IN my leg repairing my quad as we speak."

"Ah man, no way, what are you talking about?"

"You see, they have this technology here where they've perfected a way to put microscopic machines in your body and these machines do what they have told them to do. In my case, they told the bots to rebuild my vastus lateralis muscle, the big one on the outside of the thigh. So all these boots, that's what the staff calls them, boots, all these boots are programmed to gather the materials needed and then they go and frickin build me a new leg muscle. Is it awesome or what?"

"It is fa-reeking me out, that's what it is. How many of these things are in you?"

"Thirty, forty thousand, something like that. Some gather stuff, the miners, some are building the knee, the builders, and some are even calling the shots, the directors. It's a damn jobsite in there. The progress I'm making, I'll be ready to play by the ALDS.

"Whoa, there is no way, dude. Yorkey tells me Lewis said 6 months. Lewis says you are done for the year."

"That's what they think. That's why I had you talk to Yorkey. I wanted to see how he felt about me, and I think I found out. All these years as long as I'm producing, I'm his best friend. But now that he thinks I'm injured, I'm useless to him. Well, he's got a big shock coming and it's going to hit him right in the pocket. I'm going to show him and all those other jerks exactly who Brad

Dickson is. I'm going to show them I'm a miracle, that I'm Superman."

"What's that bookie's name in Vegas you work with? Tony something or other, yeah?"

Chapter 15

By day 8, Brad was making phenomenal progress. He was scoring as high or higher on all the physical therapy tests than he had in a couple of years. Each day, each session brought new plateaus. The treadmill tests were now flat out runs. Where just a few days ago he could barely walk, he was now doing 7 minute miles, one after the other. His leg felt strong and more limber. He started weight lifting sessions on day 6. He started out fairly light but could now squat 300 pounds, nearly as much as he could in his best years. Even the therapists could not believe the progress he was making.

"Mr. Dickson, you are progressing faster than I could ever have imagined," commented Dr. Gupta that morning, "I did not take into consideration, nor understood the value of your lifelong level of top physical fitness. Add to that your amazingly swift healing ability and you have exceeded our most optimistic projections. Plus, we believe the nanobots, being in such a healthy environment, are also performing better than expected. They are learning from your body's naturally fast healing process, and as a result, they too are achieving a far greater level of efficiency than projections would indicate. The MRI results from yesterday show the muscle is 90% rebuilt. We project nanobot shutdown will occur sometime late Tuesday, with complete evacuation occurring sometime over the next two days, ending by Thursday, the 2nd of October. By the time you leave us, you will surpass anything we would have hoped for. I suspect your PT ratings will be higher than any you've ever achieved?"

"I think you may be right, doc," Brad replied confidently, "I cannot remember the last time I did a seven minute mile on the treadmill, let alone 10 of them. I know I'll be ready for the playoffs next week."

Brad was feeling really good. Earlier in the day Marisa had arrived. She was astonished by how happy Brad seemed and could not believe her eyes while she watched him run on the treadmill.

"It's a miracle Brad," she said, as she wiped the sweat from his forehead between sprint sets, "I would never have believed it if I hadn't seen it myself."

Brad eagerly showed her around the facility. They even popped into the control center where Brad read the current counts on his bots.

Miners – 32140 and 282

Builders – 4315 and 49

Directors – 194 and 3

"Those are counts of the three types of machines working in my body," he explained to her, "the first column are the active nanobots and the second column represents malfunctions of one sort or another. Over the past 5 days, there have only been a miniscule number of malfunctions creating a very limited loss of productivity. A far better rate than my doctors had projected."

"Loss of productivity? I don't understand."

"The nanobots are machines. Sometimes they fail or malfunction and no longer are productive. That second set of numbers show how many have failed."

"Look at that screen over there," Brad pointed to the topo console, "you can see where the nanobots are at all times in my body. That dark area just above my knee where there are many blue dots is where the miners deposit the materials and the builders, the green dots, are working to create muscle tissue that they build to build up my muscle. Once they are done they will be instructed by the directors, the red dots, to leave my body. They will all march into my kidney where I'll wizz them right on out into the stool. It's absolutely unbelievable!"

"Can you feel them," she asked.

"Sometimes, when I lie perfectly still and concentrate really hard, I think I can feel them moving around my upper leg. I get kind of a twitching sensation in my knee. The techies tell me the miners are mining for materials in virtually all parts of my body, but I only think I feel them in my thigh."

"What happens when they mine all the materials they can find?"

"That will never happen. They feed me high doses of supplements in my food as well as medicine and daily intravenous drips to ensure I am producing as much natural amino acids and proteins as the miner bots need. The miners know because they have learned where to find the supply of ingredients needed to continue the process. The nurses monitor my blood and do other tests to keep track of those things. If my counts get low, they give me something to increase production. They are monitoring every aspect of the process. And, as I told you on the phone, when the job is done, they will all pack up and go home, or down the drain as it were."

"It gives me the creeps," Marisa said, looking down at his leg, trying to see some movement of the little machines he was describing.

"It's nothing more than modern science giving my body's natural healing mechanism a little help. The bots are doing the job in days it would take my body months to do on its own."

"Have you talked to Bob or Mr. Yorkey about possibly returning for the playoffs?"

"No, and I don't want you to say anything to them either. When the time comes, they, along with everybody else, will know. I want this to be the surprise of the season."

They left the control room and Brad showed her around the facility, where he received the MRIs, where he ate, where he had blood drawn. She was impressed by the cleanliness of the facility and how nice all the people were. She was not impressed with Dr. Gupta.

"He gives me the creeps," she said when they were back in his room, alone. "He just seems to be interested in his experiments and his own accomplishments. I don't think he cares about your health, he just wants to prove to the world that his nanobots work and he alone has advanced science and mankind."

"Don't be too hard or judgmental, Mar. I'm the one who talked him into trying his techniques on a human. He didn't want to and in fact turned me down numerous times before my charm finally won him over. Like what it's going to do to you." With that he put his arm around her waist and lowered her to his bed.

Chapter 16

Marisa stayed the night. They arose early to spend maximum time together before she had to leave for the airport. Breakfast went too quickly and soon the cabbie arrived at Nano Robotics to take Marisa to the airport to catch her flight back home to Detroit.

As they stood in the company's foyer, arms embraced, Brad gave her one last squeeze.

She looked up and said, "I'll miss you babe, can't wait to see you in a few days."

"Me too. Just three more days here and I'll be back in your arms, stronger and better than ever."

"It will be pretty hard for you to top last night."

A big smiled grew on Brad's face, "Be sure to keep mum on my whereabouts. If Yorkey or the reporters or anyone else asks you where I'm at, just tell them I'm rehabbing and will be home soon."

"I will babe. I love you."

"I love you too."

He opened the door for her and followed her down the walk to the waiting cab. The driver had the right rear door open and Marisa slid down into the seat, and the driver closed the door behind her. She rolled down the window and reached out her hand to Brad. He gave her bag to the cabbie and grabbed her hand in his. Their eyes shared an intense stare for several long moments.

The driver threw her bag in the trunk, slid in behind the wheel, and oblivious to their bonding, pulled away from the curb. Their handhold broke, but not their gaze, as the cab shrunk away from the curb.

After watching the cab disappear around the corner, Brad turned toward the main entrance and thought to himself, let's see what Superman can do today, and walked briskly, with no hint of a limp, back into the building.

He quickly changed into his workout gear, a Tigers World Series Championship hooded sweatshirt, baggy grey sweat pants and New Balance 610 tennis shoes. The first workout of the day would be on the treadmill. Alice, the lead therapist whom he'd gotten to know these past few days, was waiting with clipboard in hand and stethoscope around her neck.

"Morning, Alice, what's it gonna be this morning?"

"Good morning, Brad. Today I'm going to start you off with 5 minutes of warm up at 4 and a half miles an hour, then I'm going to work you on some sprint drills, 30 seconds at 7 miles an hour, followed by 30 seconds at 10 miles an hour. I'll just keep alternating that until you either say stop or your heartbeat goes above 180, whichever comes first."

"Piece of cake. That's easy, Alice, ha ha. Get it?"

She didn't. "If you don't get to 180, I want to work you on some endurance runs right on top of the sprints. I've got to say Brad, you are really challenging us to come up with a plan every day. Every time we advance your targets you just plow right through them with no apparent effort. It's just amazing how fast you have risen to your current level. You have already exceeded the targets we had set for you for the entire rehab program."

'Thanks to you, my dear, I am feeling stronger, faster, and younger than I've felt in years. Let's get started." He hopped on the tread and Alice started up the machine. He breezed through the warm up and did the circuits one after the other, neither sweating nor breathing hard.

After 60 minutes, Alice stopped the machine. "OK Brad, you've done it again," she faked disappointment, "let's see how you do with some endurance circuits."

She set the machine for 9 miles per hour, and motioned Brad to hop back on.

"What was my pulse at the end of the sprints?"

"One thirty, barely in the aerobic zone. Come on Brad, you're not even trying," she joked.

Brad jumped on and began the run. After another hour, Alice gave up, "That's enough, we're done for now." She made some notes, added his 135 heart rate on the clipboard in her hand, and shaking her head, left the room.

Brad wiped the small beads of sweat that had formed from his forehead with a towel. He was not even panting after a full two hours on the treadmill. He looked down at his injured leg. The muscles above the knee bulged out with a pronounced valley between them like a Tour De France cyclist. He looked from leg to leg; the left leg definitely was bigger around the quadriceps area. But the right leg was also bigger. All the physical therapy had strengthened his good leg too. He did his best bicep flex for the mirror, grabbed a towel, and went to his room to shower.

On the way, as was his daily habit, he peeked into the control room. The room was crowded. Usually there were only two technicians on duty but now there were the two technicians, Drs. Gupta and Childress, and another man he did not know. They were staring intently at the nanobot count screen until he opened the door and all eyes looked quickly to him, then at each other. Brad sensed nervousness pervading the group.

"What's up gang?" Brad coolly walked over to the screen they had surrounded. "What's the score today?"

"Mr. Dickson," Dr. Gupta took a step away from the others, toward Brad, grabbed his arm and distanced he and Brad from the rest of the group. "There has been a noticeable drop in the number of active directors, that is all. Yesterday there were still 194 functioning directors and this morning during your workout, 4 directors ceased to function properly. This is the first time we've had director failure since the initial injection. But let me assure you, there is no need for concern, because it is still well within the safety parameters we have established. We are convinced it is just a result of your vigorous workouts. We expect to lose nanobots at this stage as they have been working hard and their task is nearly finished. In fact, the time is near for a slowdown and general shutdown of material gathering and the miners will start migrating towards your kidneys for flush out. We anticipate this will start occurring sometime today or early tomorrow. The number of active miners, however, will not drop until evacuation begins. Soon after we see the miner evacuation, the builders will start to

88

wrap things up as well. That phase will be characterized by the builders moving in ever expanding concentric circles which signifies they have completed the core tissue building process. They have instructions to check the periphery area to ensure the new cells have been bonded properly to the adjacent tissue. As a reminder of what we had discussed earlier, the last group, the directors, will be the last to move. At that point in the process they will traverse your entire body, rather slowly to pick up and redirect any miner bot still doing its task. This phase will go on for a day or so until the directors have accounted for all the other bots, whereby they too will start making the migration toward the evacuation zone. Perhaps if they detect any corrections or unfinished areas as they are making their inspection, they may summons some builders and miners back to active status to make the needed repairs. What we are discussing at the moment is why the directors have lost members within the past two hours. There is no alarm, we just were not anticipating this event.

We are still at a 99% safety rate. Besides, the work is nearly finished and the work left to do does not require the full complement of directors anyway. Each director is programmed with the entire program. Losing any one director will cause the remaining ones to take up the slack as it were. With little left to do, this is easily accomplished. In fact, in the absolute worst case scenario, one director could finish the task."

"What if there were no directors left to finish the job," Brad inquired loudly. The others turned their attention to Brad. He tried to read their reaction to his question, but to a man, they revealed nothing.

89

"In that extreme case," it was Dr. Childress who spoke, "we would abandon the project. Send the command ultrasonically to the workers to proceed to the evacuation area. The non-functional directors in your body would gradually be absorbed into your tissue and eventually pass out through your skin. But I assure you, that can't happen. We've not had to abort a mission since the very early days when we were still trying to develop the command language."

Brad supposed this was true. He had no reason to doubt Dr. Childress, after all, everything has gone according to plan, even better, so far.

"I had a great physical therapy session today," said Brad changing the subject, much to the delight of the others. "I didn't even get winded. I think I am ready to play ball, what do you think?"

"Your recovery has been remarkable. We were confident of the capabilities of our nanobots, but we did not anticipate the role your athletic conditioning and powers of healing would factor in to the equation," said Dr. Gupta taking the lead once again. "We also believe you are ready to return to your activities."

"While all this rehab has been good for my injured leg, the right leg has had to do just as much work and feels stronger too."

"That's something we did not anticipate either Brad, but a nice serendipity, wouldn't you say?" asked Dr. Childress.

"I will talk to you gentlemen later, I need to go blow some of this stink off," and as he said it, Brad turned toward the door. As his head turned, he glanced up at the topology screen and saw a consolidation of miner bots around the area above his right knee.

90

Hmmm, he thought to himself, they must be looking for materials. As he walked down the hall it occurred to him, those were not miners, they were green. He was sure of it.

Chapter 17

The day consisted of three more physical therapy sessions, blood lettings and another MRI. Brad was getting pretty tired of this routine, especially the bloodletting. He had never liked needles or giving blood samples and was becoming extra irritated at the frequency he was asked to do this.

He had nearly forgotten about the bots in his right leg until he was lying on his bed after dinner reading a Sports Illustrated on his iPad IX. Surely they were miners, he thought to himself, what would builders be doing in his good leg? He couldn't concentrate on the article he was reading about the pennant race he was not in, so he threw the iPad on the bed, opened the door, and started toward the control center. When he got there he put his hand on the knob and turned. It would not turn, it was locked. He rattled it some more, but no good, it was indeed locked. He knocked on the door but heard nothing from within. Strange, he thought, this door had never been locked before. But he also realized he had never gone into the control center this late. Maybe they just lock it at night because there's no one there. Wait, 'no one there?' He had been told there would always be two people minimum in that room to monitor the bots in his body. He put his ear against the door and listened for a few moments, but heard no activity from within.

Concerned, he swiftly walked to the security area near the front lobby. A guard he recognized was on duty. He was a middle aged man, not particularly intelligent looking, nor looking like he was particularly interested in doing his job properly.

"Hi," Brad said, "pretty boring tonight, eh?"

"Yes sir, it's always pretty quiet around here after hours. Usually, the only ones I have to talk to are the lab rats when I make my rounds. It's nice to have a real human around. Maybe we'll have more people like you from now on."

"Perhaps. Hey, I was bored and wanted to see my topo, but the door is locked to the control room."

"Yes sir, that room stays locked every night as soon as the last technician leaves and gives me the word. Since you've been here, up until tonight, they've been in there around the clock, but Peter left about eight-thirty and told me to lock it. Said he'd be back after getting a bite."

"They always let me in when I want, can we just go take a quick look?"

"I don't think I'm supposed to let you in there. Before you, they always kept it locked, every night, just because they must have some costly equipment in there. They didn't tell me no different for you."

"But, like I say...., I didn't catch your name?"

"Bill."

"Yeah, Bill, like I was saying, they've always let me in there. It's nothing special, just a couple of screens with dots and numbers. Not rocket science."

"I've never been in the room."

"Would you like to see what's in there?"

93

"Well, you know, they didn't say NOT to let anybody in and I guess if you've been in there before I don't see any harm."

He reached for the keys on the desk and led Brad to the control room. Bill jiggled the key into to the door and turned the knob.

Brad impulsively walked to the count screen

Miners 32138 – 284

Builders 4314 – 50

Directors 188 – 9

The miners and builders are pretty stable, he thought, but with two more directors lost since earlier today, Brad started to get an uneasy feeling about it.

He walked over to the topo screen and confirmed what he had suspected earlier, the green builders were in his right knee, and it appeared to be more of them than he remembered from earlier in the day. As he watched, he saw more builders moving away from his left knee, up through his groin and down to his right knee. It reminded him of an ant colony he had watched in the woods near his house when he was a kid. They had marched single file, one behind the other, following what appeared to be a haphazard path that zigged and zagged around roots and dead leaves. But each ant following one another, like good soldiers marching into battle. The nanobots' path zigged and zagged up his left leg, and down his right. The area above his left knee noticeable less dense with the green dots of the builders and red dots of the directors. All of the blue dot miners appeared to be either on their way to the right knee, or on their way away from it. All red dots were at the left leg.

"Jeepers, what are all those specks on the screen," Bill asked.

"Those are the nanobots that are in my body."

"It looks like an army of them."

"There are a bunch of them in me, alright."

"What do the little green ones do?"

"They're the ones that do the building."

"Dang, it sure looks like they're an army mounting an attack."

That's what it looked like to Brad, too.

Chapter 18

Brad didn't sleep a wink all night. What could be going on? Why were the builders moving over to his good leg? Why did it look like the directors were clueless, staying on the left knee, overseeing nothing? Why were the miners continuing to gather materials, and why were they bringing the materials to the right knee? Why were directors dying?

He sprang from the bed when he heard footsteps in the hallway. He threw the door open just in time to see one of the technicians enter the control room and shut the door. He raced down the hall and grabbed the handle, it was locked. He began knocking on the door furiously.

The technician, opened the door, with a look of horror on his face, eyes wide open.

"Uh, morning Brad, er, I mean, Mr. Dickson, how are you today?"

"Let's forget the pleasantries, what the hell is going on?"

"What, what, do you mean Mr. Dickson?"

"I mean, what the hell is going on with the nanobots. Look, look at that screen," he yelled, pointing at the topo screen. "Why are they all going over to my right knee? There's nothing wrong with my right knee, there's no reason for them to be there. So tell me why they are there?"

"I, I don't know, I mean, I'm not sure I should say, what I'm saying is, perhaps Dr. Gupta should talk to you."

"Where is he?"

"I don't think he's here yet, let me go ask security."

"No, you're not going anywhere. Why don't you call security instead?"

The technician picked up the phone and dialed the security desk. "Hi, Joe here. I'm in the control room with Mr. Dickson and he is wondering where Dr. Gupta is. He'd like to speak to him."

"Uh, huh, yes, I think he is, yes. I don't know how. Just the two of us, yes. Thank you, we'll wait right here."

"Dr. Gupta will be right down," said the shaken technician as he moved further away from Brad.

A few minutes later, they heard the sound of footsteps, and Dr. Gupta entered the room, along with two security guards.

"Good morning, Mr. Dickson how are you this morning?"

Looking at the doctor then at the two guards, then back at Dr. Gupta, Brad said, "What the hell is going on here? Why the guards?"

"Mr. Dickson, please calm down. There is no cause for alarm. I was about to come talk to you when Joe called the security desk."

"Come talk to me about what, the bots in my right leg?"

Dr. Gupta shot an icy glance at the technician, who shrugged his shoulders. "As a matter of fact yes, how do you know about the builder migration?"

"I saw it on the topo screen yesterday. Then last night I saw where more had moved there, and the miners are supplying them with materials. And directors are dying. What is happening?"

"I assure you, there is no cause for alarm. We have been monitoring the migration for two days. We did not say anything to you because we were not sure what has happened. What I do suspect is it appears that the miners, during their foraging through the body, brought back information they shared with the directors and builders that the vastus lateralis in your right leg has some imperfection as well. The bots are programmed to rebuild and repair muscle tissue in the vastus lateralis. It appears they are doing just that, making the muscle in your right leg just as strong and perfect as they have made the one in your left. The construction process being performed is identical to the one just finished on your bad leg. They are doing what they were designed to do, no more no less. If anything, the outcome is you will have two brand new vastus lateralii. An even better outcome than you had hoped for, yes?"

Brad was confused. He was sure the procedure had gone wrong, but what Dr. Gupta was saying made sense. If he could have two good legs, it would make him an even better, stronger ball player. "What then will happen when they are done making my right leg muscle perfect?"

"That is a reasonable question, Brad." The doctor began to rub his hands together unconsciously, "We believe we have made a mistake in the command sequence in that we did not specify to only do the left quad. We input all the proper parameters to build the muscle, but neglected to say 'just the one on the left'. The bots found another vastus imperfection, examined it and created a plan to fix it. We believe when that project is done, the original program sequence will continue and the bots will cease and proceed to the evacuation as I have described before. In the meantime, we will monitor their activities and be ready to react as needed. I suggest it's a good thing, unexpected, but good. You will benefit greatly from our mistake."

"How long do you anticipate it will take for them to be done?" Brad asked.

"With your left leg we had to start from scratch. The miners had to prospect, and bring materials to the work site. The builders had to identify where and when and how much was needed and at what time. The directors had to set up both groups, setting up lines of communication. This setup phase consumed the better part of two days. Once things were in place, the miners knew where to get materials, the builders knew where and when. After that, the process went rather quickly. I anticipate since all the bots are seasoned and with the materials being readily available, the process will still come to a close in the timeframe we originally estimated, one to two days from now. I am confident we will hit your desired schedule."

"You don't see any downside to this new development?" Brad quizzed.

"No, do you?" answered Dr. Gupta. "What is wrong with having two perfectly healthy and strong legs?"

Brad returned to his room. He paced back and forth, flexing each leg, feeling the strength they had gained, and pondering the significance of Dr. Gupta's words. This was concerning to him on the one hand, this unanticipated development. He wanted to believe the doctor this was an unexpected but positive thing, but on the other hand, he was uneasy how the men in the control room had reacted to his sudden appearance and their nervousness when Dr. Gupta was speaking. He thought he needed to get one of the technicians alone sometime later and see if there was anything the doctor was not telling him. At the moment though he was thinking how cool it would be to return even better than originally planned. The end result could mean he could easily play five or more years, adding millions to his market value.

Chapter 19

Brad went to his physical therapy session later as scheduled, but he could sense that Alice and the others were a little uptight, no, a LOT uptight during the session. There was no joking and they were all business. He also thought Alice was particularly distant. She avoided eye contact with him as he went through his routine on the treadmill.

"What's wrong Alice?" Brad finally said halfway through his endurance set. "Know something I don't know?"

"No Brad, it's just, well, it's just we heard about the problem this morning and I'm worried about you."

"Worried? But this is a good thing, yes? Dr. Gupta assured me the bots will build up my right leg muscle and then be done with their work. Both of my legs will be super strong. What's the problem in that?"

"I'm sorry I said 'problem', I didn't mean the work of the bots is a problem, I meant your confrontation with Dr. Gupta and the technicians was a problem, that's all. We were told that you blew up in the control room and that we were to stay focused today and not to initiate too much conversation with you. I think it stinks, but that's what we are supposed to do."

"Don't fret, it was nothing. I was concerned about the bots going crazy, but the explanation Dr. Gupta gave me made sense, and besides, it's for the better."

The rest of the session was conducted in silence, Brad exceeding the day's goals again.

After his shower, Brad went straight to the control room. This time the door was unlocked.

"Hi Mr. Dickson," Joe, one of the technicians Brad had befriended, said, looking up from his work when Brad entered the room, "How did your PT go this morning?"

"Kicked butt, as usual. I don't think Alice can believe what I'm able to do on her tests. She gets kind of cranky when I blow her expectations away. Me, I love it."

"Maybe she's had more on her mind this morning than usual."

"How's that?"

"Don't tell anyone I told you this but, I know Dr. Childress had a long talk with her and the others this morning about what happened earlier and he told them under no circumstance were they to tell you anything and to keep conversation with you to a minimum. I know Alice was not happy about that, I think she kind of likes you. But from what I hear, she did what she was told. Did you sense anything different?"

"Yes, she was kind of distant. I figured there was something up, but she really didn't say much. In fact none of the therapists said much to me during the session."

"Well, I'm sure things will settle down now and get back to normal."

"Speaking of normal," Brad changed subjects, "let's take a look at my boots and say what the hell they're up to."

They both turned to look at the topo screen. More blue and green bots had moved over to the right leg than he witnessed earlier.

"What percentage of greens are in the right leg now?" Brad asked.

Joe hesitated a moment, not wanting to start this conversation with Brad. "About 40%, a little more than 1700. More are headed that way though, as you can see," pointing to the continuous arch of bots moving from the left leg to the right. "The number of miners delivering material to the right leg is nearly 100%. They definitely are done on the left and are now fully committed to building up your right quad."

"Fine by me," Brad smiled, now pleased with this development, "maybe they'll fix all me mus-culls," intentionally using the Popeye pronunciation and doing a poor imitation of the sailor.

"Maybe they will," Joe echoed. "There are some green stragglers in all your muscle groups, see," he said pointing to areas in his arms and torso with a handful of green dots.

Brad leaned into the screen. Indeed there were green builder bots moving through both biceps, across his torso, down at both calves, up near his neck. They seemed to be everywhere.

"What does that mean? Why are they all over my body?" He was getting the same feeling of concern he'd had that morning.

"I'm not sure, Brad. I think because the builders are programmed to look for damage in muscle tissue, they are exploring your entire body looking for work. At least that's my theory at the moment. Since we've never done this before, I mean, on a person, I'm just guessing what's happening. Strange though that none of the director bots are in the new areas. It's as if they have lost control of

103

the project. They keep dropping out. We're down to 185 now. Not a big deal, but not what we expected."

The red director bots were indeed still concentrated in the left knee area. There were virtually no green or blue bots in the vicinity. The view was far different than what Brad had seen the first eight days.

He felt a shiver go through his body. He felt the sensation of the bots crawling up and down his arms and legs. He twisted his torso and rolled his shoulders, and still the feeling persisted. Did he imagine it, or was he feeling the bots moving around, he didn't know.

Chapter 20

Back in his room, Brad telephoned his agent, Barry, who informed him he had made contact with Tony and had made the deal with Tony that Brad had proposed. For his part, Tony was to receive 10 percent of the total amount wagered; a cool $20 million.

Barry also updated Brad on a talk he had with Al Yorkey that day. Still no commitment to the future. In fact Yorkey had suggested a reduction in salary and reducing the number of years of the contract they had already agreed upon.

"Good, well, keep me apprised of your negotiation. Yes, I'll be out of here in two days. Yes, don't say anything to Yorkey or anybody about my return. I want it to be a surprise."

After hanging up with Barry, Brad dialed Marisa.

"HI babe," she answered knowing from the caller ID display it was Brad, "How is it going today?"

"Just fine," Brad answered. He wasn't quite ready to tell her about the latest developments. "I'm exceeding their expectations every day. Just two more days and I'll be home. I can't wait, I'm getting homesick."

"I want you home too, baby," she said, hesitating for a moment, and then added, "Mr. Yorkey called today."

A frown formed on his face, "What did you tell him? You didn't tell him where I was did you?"

"Brad, come on, you're not giving me much credit. Of course I didn't tell him where you were. I just said you were consulting with doctors about your injury."

"What did he say when you told him that?"

"He said he was glad you were getting expert opinions and was eager to hear about what you had learned when you got back."

"That's all he said, that's it? He didn't try to find out what doctors I had visited, or where I was or when I'd get back?"

"No, that's all, just that. But now that I think about it, when we were about to hang up, he did ask another question, kind of weird I thought."

"What was that?"

"He asked if I liked the Cubs."

Brad hung up the phone. The Cubs? Why would he ask that? Did he know I was in Chicago? Did he have Marisa followed when she came out to visit? Was he in negotiations to trade me during the winter?

Brad dialed Barry back.

"Hey Bar, has Yorkey mentioned anything to you about the Cubs?"

"No Brad, not specifically. He always plays the game of acting like he's been talking to other owners about deals and trades, so I suppose he's mentioned the Cubs, along with just about every other ballclub. It's just his way of making it look like the players are not as valuable to him as they are. Why do you ask?"

"No particular reason. I just wonder if he knows I'm in Chicago and if he thinks I've contacted the Cubs."

When they hung up, Brad looked at himself in the mirror. He could visibly see the larger definition of both quads. His left one still looked slightly larger than the right, but the right one was as well-developed as ever. As he was staring at his right thigh, he was sure he could feel the nanos in there, doing their work. He did a couple of squats and a big smile formed on his face. He felt as if he had been lifted back up by an invisible force, not his own power.

Chapter 21

"Good morning, Brad." Alice had the treadmill wiped down and had the oxygen mask in her hand when Brad entered the physical therapy room. "Today we are going to see how far you can go, are you ready for it?"

"Ready as ever, sweetheart. I feel like I could run back to Michigan today."

"I might just have you do that," she said as she placed the mask over his head, adjusting the straps. She attached the electrodes to his torso and legs and motioned him to the treadmill machine.

"I'm going to start you with some rapid intervals and then a long sprint, as long as you can go. Either you say 'when' or when your heartbeat gets to 220, whichever comes first."

"Piece of cake," he replied.

The machine started up, and Brad hopped on. Gradually she increased the speed until he was doing 12 miles an hour. Alice would manually back it off to 10 miles an hour every three minutes. This went on for 10 intervals. Brad's heart rate was hovering around 120 at the faster speed, slowing back down to 110 during the slowdown. "Incredible" was the only word Alice could muster. A word she had muttered a hundred times in the past week. For his part, Brad was extremely pleased. He felt as if he were standing still. His legs had no burn and they snapped into each stride effortlessly.

"Now it's time to get serious," Alice said as she reached over to adjust the program on the apparatus.

"Were you talking to me, I was napping." He shot her a sidelong glance and raised his brows.

"I'm bumping it up to 15 miles an hour and I'm going to leave it there until you cry uncle," she challenged.

"I hope you weren't planning to do anything today, because you are going to be here a looooong time."

"We'll see."

The machine sped up and Brad easily settled into the new pace. His mind drifted back to the time he had first put on a baseball uniform. He was just 4 years old........

Every night after work, his dad would get out their gloves and a ball and play catch with him. He recalled the endless hours they would play. His dad taught him how to develop speed by using his whole body to throw; first planting his right foot, then pivoting, bringing his torso around and finally bringing his right hand past his ear, releasing the ball at the proper time and the all-important follow through to hone the accuracy of the throw. He would work with him for hours to perfect this technique. Brad remembered when he played with his friends, how they would use the wrong leg to throw from, or not turn their body, using only their arm to throw it weakly. None seemed to have the accuracy that Brad had developed from the hours of working with his dad.

It was also easy for him to catch a ball. Often, his young friends lacked the coordination to do it properly. He instinctively seemed to know where to stand and where to put his glove and was especially adept at shagging fly balls. No matter how high the ball went or how far he had to run, he had a sense of where he needed to be to make the catch. His father had drilled it into him to close his fist on his glove hand and place his throwing hand over the outside of the mitt to prevent the ball from popping out.

The little league coaches were well aware of his abilities by the time he was old enough to join. They were all eager to pick him for their team. He was the first kid picked that first year, and the lucky coach, Mr. Lake, he remembered, had to do very little teaching with Brad, because he already had the skills.

He remembered the other kids on the team didn't seem to understand the basic dynamics of how to throw or catch the ball. He even helped Mr. Lake teach them the proper method, but it was above the heads and coordination capability of most of them.

To complete the baseball trifecta, he was also a gifted batter. Maybe not gifted, but certainly well-schooled. He enjoyed playing catch with his dad but got the most enjoyment when they worked on hitting. The tinny sound of the ball hitting the aluminum bat when he hit it square, told him the ball was going to sail a long way. His dad pitched to him at a speed he wouldn't see from his competitors until he was a teenager. When he batted against pitchers his own age, the ball would come in nice and slow so he could hit it a mile. He learned early on how to watch the ball's spin and learned to anticipate the trajectory based on the speed and direction of the spin. His Dad would throw a curve or slider, and soon Brad could hit these as easily as a fastball.

Each year, he would surpass his achievements of the previous year. The pitchers his age were no match for his well-developed hand/eye coordination.

By the time he was 9, he played on a regional traveling all star team. It was made up of the best 9-11 year olds in the county. Brad was, of course, the star. He began to pitch that year, and added numerous no hitters to his already impressive batting feats. His team was undefeated going into the Little League World Series, where they reached the finals but lost against a team from Japan that featured some really big kids. There was controversy about the ages of the Japanese players, but it was never proven they were too old and Brad's team bitterly conceded the championship. It was his first taste of disappointment on the ball field and that feeling would carry him to greater achievements his entire life. In a rare repeat visit to the World Series the next year, his team got revenge by beating a different Japanese group 13-0, when Brad threw a 2 hitter and knocked in 5 runs that included a pair of home runs.

After that, it was the seniors, Connie Mack, and then American Legion ball. At each level, he would draw attention with his hitting and pitching. During his year in American Legion, the stands would be packed to watch him as he tore up the league with an unheard of .504 batting average, 27 home runs, 3 no hitters, and 173 strike outs. There would be standing room only on the days he pitched, and he rarely disappointed. The local newspaper had a running column called the Brad Watch, where his achievements were duly chronicled after each game. He became a local celebrity as he was interviewed numerous times by local and national newspaper and television news teams. He had hundreds of letters from just about every college in the country that had a baseball team. His parents fielded calls nearly every day from big league scouts and many colleges. Through it all, Brad stayed pretty well grounded. His parents, especially his dad, made sure he concentrated on improving his skills and making his statements on the ball field, and not into a microphone.

He started for his high school team as an 8th grader. Although he struggled at first, by the 5th game into the season he was seeing the faster pitches just fine and ended that year with a .314 batting average, despite playing against kids 5 years older. His high school team enjoyed success due primarily to Brad's skills at the plate and on the mound. By his sophomore year, the team was ranked number one in the state, and did not lose a game for those three years either in the regular season or the championships. Brad was voted the MVP of his conference, and the state tournament, and unanimously named captain of the all-state elite team the last two years of high school.

He remembered during his senior year, competition for his talents was intense between major league clubs as well as colleges. He was picked number 1 in the 2005 draft, as a junior. The press ridiculed the Dodgers for drafted him as a 17 year old, but in the end, he stayed in school and led his team to its third consecutive championship.

His parents were very supportive of the decision he had made to go to college instead of going pro, despite leaving a $22 million dollar signing bonus on the table. They knew, as he knew, that one freak accident, one bad slide, one awkward pitch could end his playing days and leave him with nothing, so they insisted he get a college education.

The college game proved as easy to excel in as had any of the previous levels he had played at. Playing for Texas on the national stage, Brad quickly became the prospect of the future. Despite his immense talent and gaudy numbers, he stuck it out and earned his degree, graduating with a Bachelor's Degree in communications.

The major league owners were licking their chops to get their hands on him, and as it happened, the Tigers had just finished their 4th consecutive losing record in '08 going a pathetic 74-88. That horrible record proved their great fortune as they traded with Washington to chose Brad Number 1 in the 2009 draft.

It was a well-known story: The team owner, Albert Yorkey, had bought the club in 2007. He could not have had better luck. Yorkey had made his fortune as the founder of the Internet virtual reality company, Oogle. He had corrected guessed the new field would take off and became the de facto leader in providing virtual experiences for millions using real life combat games for the teens and sexual encounters for the adults. His empire accounted for 10% of all revenue earned on the internet. The Tigers had been a losing franchise for years and the previous owners, the Ford family, had been hemorrhaging money both from the club and their declining car company. Yorkey came along at an ideal time, both to the relief of the Ford family and the Tiger faithful. Despite the commissioner's initial reluctance to allow ownership to the violence and soft porn king, the other club owners finally convinced him that Yorkey was a brilliant businessman the league and the Tigers needed. Yorkey set about changing the atmosphere of the club house immediately. He fired the GM and all the coaches and brought in a new team. He bribed his GM, Don Hanratty, from the Marlins, to the tune of $24 million per year, and was personally involved in hiring Bob Startlin, his staff, and all the minor league managers and coaches with the recommendations given to him by Hanratty, who himself had built a reputation and empire at the Florida team, by winning 3 of the previous 5 World Series before jumping to the Tigers.

Brad remembered when he first met with Yorkey. He was flown to Yorkey's home on St. John in the Virgin Islands. Brad had seen some big homes, but nothing like the one that Yorkey owned above Hawksnest Bay. The home was build on the side of a sheer cliff. Brad had been picked up by one of Yorkey's bodyguards at the St. Thomas Airport, driven in a brand new Mercedes jeep to the other end of the island, where they boarded a car ferry for the 30 minute trip to St. John. There, they weaved their way through the traffic and pedestrian congestion of Cruz Bay, and climbed the hill with the million-dollar view of the bay, towards Yorkey's summer home. On the way, the jeep, driving on the left, as they had always done on this island, passed many pickup trucks with colorful canvas tops over the beds, which contained bench seats on each side. The benches were occupied by lightly dressed tourists returning from the north shore beaches, heading back to their rented homes or cruise ships waiting at Charlotte Amalie.

After a 5 mile ride through dense forest, winding roads, hairpin turns and nearly being run off the road by more than one taxi truck, they turned into a gated entrance down a narrow lane and burst out upon a huge, pastel pink home. The roofs of the four sections were terra cotta tile, in a gable style. Each section of the structure had a main floor supported by brick archways. From the driveway, Brad could see an infinity pool under the nearest arch, and what appeared to be a garden under the next. As they hopped out of the jeep, a native man rushed out of the gate and reached into the back to grab Brad's bag. The walk to the house was on clear glass tile, three tiles wide. Each tile had a tropical scene underneath. Some depicted waterfront and beach scenes and some showed landscapes of lush vegetation. They walked through an arched heavy wooden door. In this entry room were marble tables on the sides and an aquarium built into one wall. The aquarium had hundreds of tropical fish of every hue. The opposite wall was a large glass window with a view of the entire Hawksnest beach, with the island of Jost Van Dyke in the distance. The floor appeared to be bamboo and a circular rug of African origin covered all but the edges of the floor. Through the entryway, they entered the central room of the main house. The ceiling was 20 feet high where two large fiber leafed fans were rotating slowly. On the walls were paintings that appeared to Brad to be very old. The furniture in this room was primarily leather, with three couches and handful of oversized settees. At the far end of the room was a wide staircase that rose halfway up then split in two and wound around like a spiral staircase to join up with the second floor. It reminded Brad of an old Southern mansion he had seen on one of his Texas team's swings through Mississippi. The bodyguard, Eric, motioned for Brad to sit in one of the chairs and left the room.

After a few minutes, Brad saw Mr. Yorkey for the first time. A man in his early fifties, with thick short black hair, well-built, stocky, wearing a short-sleeved Sloop Jones tie dye Oxford, khaki shorts, and Birkenstock sandals. He was on the second floor balcony and descended the stairs.

"Good morning Brad. I am so glad you are here. How was your ride over from St Thomas?"

Brad quickly rose to his feet, knocking the chair back a little as he did so, "Mr. Yorkey, it's a pleasure to meet you, sir." Quickly spanning the distance and holding his hand out to a firm handshake from Yorkey. "The ride was fine. Eric took good care of me."

"It appears you did not get run over by one of our crazy taxi drivers. That's good."

"There were a couple of close calls, sir, but Eric saved us just in time."

"Please Brad, Call me Al, all my friends do and I hope we will become close friends in the coming years."

"I do too, Mr. York.., I mean, Al."

"Sit back down Brad. Would you like a drink; tea, beer, rum?" As he spoke, a beautiful blond-haired girl barely older than Brad appeared at the doorway, ready for Brad's response.

"I think it's a little early for rum. Could I have an iced tea please?" he directly at the girl, smiling, he added, "sweetened."

"I will have what Brad is having," Yorkey directed and the girl disappeared.

Looking back to Brad, Yorkey said, "How do you like my little hacienda?"

"It's awesome, Al. I've never been in a room in a house this big in my life."

"I had this place built in 2000; I bought the property in 1999, and tore down the existing house that had been damaged in hurricane Georges in 1998. Took us two years to complete it. It has 10 bedrooms, 8 bathrooms, an infinity pool, 8-car garage, a movie theater, a complete workout room and a 10,000 bottle wine cellar. It was a hassle getting all the materials out here, and getting decent labor on the island, but we managed to get it complete in one year less than my original architect had projected. After I fired him, my new architect got the job done in record time. He was well motivated." A slow smile formed on his face, "This place has everything I want, a place to relax, a place to work out, a place to entertain. You know what it doesn't have?"

"No sir, I don't."

"It doesn't have a Commissioner's Trophy. See that shelf over there by the waterfall", he said, pointing at a marble shelf, built into the concave wall next to a two-story aqua blue waterfall. "That was built to display the trophy, one that I haven't gotten yet, but hope to have soon with your help."

"Sir, that's something I would like to have too."

"My teams have not been up to the task. We've spent money but have not gotten a return on that money yet. Do you think you can bring a title to Detroit?"

Brad looked out over the aqua blue water of Hawksnest Bay. A sailboat was making its way west, using the light breeze at its back. Mr. Yorkey seemed to be a man who usually got what he wanted.

117

Brad knew this was a tall order and Mr. Yorkey was placing all his faith on Brad's abilities. Brad had never been on a team that had not won the top prize. He looked back at Mr. Yorkey, and calmly said, "I guarantee it."

"That's what I wanted to hear. I have heard many good things about you young man, and if half of the stories are true, I'm certain we will bring a World Series Championship to the Motor City."

The rest of the visit Brad was pampered as he had never imagined. He received a daily massage. He had his own chauffeur who drove him around the island. He was always accompanied by at least two of the most beautiful women he had ever seen. One day they would snorkel at Trunk Bay, scuba dive at Leinster Bay, or drive to Coral Bay at the other end of the island to eat lunch or dinner at Skinny Leg's. Then the next day he would start the day with another full massage, then off they'd go on a new adventure; sailing to the British Virgins, exploring the Baths on Virgin Gorda, or hobnobbing with cruisers on tiny Cooper Island. At times, they would go out on a sunset sail on Mr. Yorkey's 54 foot Irwin sailboat. Most nights they would go into Cruz Bay and party half the night away. During the week he was there, Brad never saw Mr. Yorkey again. But he knew he was still there because the staff was always talking about Mr. Yorkey's whereabouts and where they needed to be at certain times. Eric would have discussions with Brad's driver out of earshot, but he had the feeling Eric was relaying orders from Mr. Yorkey or getting updates about Brad's comings and goings.

It was the best week of Brad's life, for sure. He was certain this was the life he wanted.

On the seventh day Eric had interrupted his massage and announced that Mr. Yorkey had gone back to the states, and Brad should get ready to head for home too. On the ride to the airport, Eric's phone rang, and he handed it to Brad.

"Hi Brad, sorry I got busy during your stay and didn't get a chance to visit more with you. But I think we communicated well enough. We both want the same things, right?"

"You bet, Al. I'm on board."

"Good. When you get back, I want you to come to Detroit as soon as possible so you can meet the team and get to work. Have your agent get in touch with Don Hanratty and work out the details of your contract."

And that was that. When he got back, Barry called and said the contract had been put together with the Tigers giving him everything he asked for, $120 million over five years, plus all the various incentives Barry could think of. There had been a grand total of 2 hours of discussion before the agreement was inked.

The early days were frustrating for Brad, but he started strong, played for only a brief time in the minors, delivered everything he had promised to Mr. Yorkey that day on St. John and within 3 years, Don Hanratty, with Mr. Yorkey's money had put together a pennant contender. The breakthrough for Brad came during the 2011 season, where Brad batted .341, hit 37 home runs and drove in 131 runs. They barely missed the World Series in a 7 game ALCS series with the Angels. The next year, they took it all.

119

Brad was the reigning MVP and riding on top of the world.

It was about that time the second great Internet bust started. Hackers and attackers from third world countries and organized cyber gangs made it virtually impossible to do business on the Internet. People became reluctant to even use it for email. All online commerce sites suffered huge dips in visits and only the ones that had brick and mortar stores were able to maintain healthy profits. Companies such as Oogle, which only did business on the internet, suffered the greatest losses. No longer able to fuel his team with internet profits, Mr. Yorkey was forced to tighten his belt and shed some of his high-priced players. Brad's contract was due to expire at the end of the season and Brad wondered where he'd be playing the next year. But Mr. Yorkey somehow came up with the money that Barry had requested, although the negotiation this time was not as friendly and dragged on for three months in the off-season. There was still enough talent under contract for the Tigers to prosper and they added two more trophies to Mr. Yorkey's collection, which was now displayed in his Detroit office, since he had to sell the home in St. John the year before. But after the contract renegotiation, there was a big difference in the relationship Brad had with Mr. Yorkey. Brad would see him in the clubhouse and try to start up a conversation, but Yorkey always seemed to be in a hurry and never had time to stop and chat, as he had done in the early Oogle glory days. Once during the season when Brad was going through a mild slump, he was called into Mr. Yorkey's office. When he walked in, seated in front of the desk was Bob Startlin and Don Hanratty with grim looks on their faces and Mr. Yorkey staring out the window. As the door shut behind

Brad, Yorkey turned around and motioned Brad to sit in the remaining chair in front of his desk and sat down.

"Gentlemen, I do not have to tell you the precarious state of the ballclub. Oogle is losing money daily and our fans are becoming complacent about our team and its mediocre record this year so far. I can't say I blame them. Would you pay $150 to come see the lackluster performances I've been watching now for the past six weeks? I sure as hell would be mad and I don't blame them at all. For years I've poured millions and millions of dollars into the pockets of our ballplayers, digging deeper and deeper to get even better athletes. It's only because of the sheer size of my wealth that has afforded you the ability to field a competitive team, Don."

Hanratty fidgeted in his chair.

He continued, "And Bob, some of the lineups and pitching changes I've witnessed make me wonder if you or any of your coaches give a damn anymore. Do you?" he blasted.

"Of course Mr. Yorkey, it's just we are going through......"

He didn't allow Startlin to finish, "And the play of our superstars is lackluster and uninspired at best. You Brad, You haven't had a home run in three weeks and you average is below the Mendoza line for the month."

Brad seethed, "You know what Al, that's crap, that's pure crap to talk about a short period in a very long season and decide that's how it is. I've had slumps that lasted longer and still ended up getting your precious trophy, not once, not twice, but three times. I filled your damn stadium year after year with hotdog eating, beer guzzling fans buying overpriced Brad Dickson shirts and Brad

121

Dickson autographed baseballs, so get off my case. Maybe if you'd loosen your wallet a little and get me some help, we could make a push for the pennant again."

Yorkey's face reddened, "Loosen my wallet? Is that it? Is that going to give you back the skills I'm paying top dollar for already? Is that going to hide your lack of productivity? Is that going to cause you to start hitting home runs again? I think you should stop worrying about my wallet and start working harder on your game."

"I give it 100% every time I'm on the field. I don't need this crap", as Brad said this he bolted up, knocking the chair over and stomped out of the room, slamming the door hard.

The team improved after that, even won 9 in a row at one point, but finished out of the playoffs for the first time in years. Brad had gotten out of the slump, still finishing with a .307 average, but he sprained an ankle in August and went on the DL for the first time in his career. He had sensed a slip in his body's ability to bounce back. He was losing his love for the game too, so he couldn't blame it entirely on his bad ankle.

"45 minutes Brad, heart rate 115, respiratory, 65." Alice said, bringing Brad back to the present, "how are you feeling?"

"Am I running?" he joked, "I'd nearly forgotten you had this baby cranked up. I'm feeling fine. I was just thinking how much I'm in love with you."

"Really? Is it because I put you through so much pain?"

"Pain, what pain? I feel good. I feel very good. I honestly think I could do this all day."

Returning to his thoughts, Brad realized the closeness he had felt to Yorkey all those years as they were climbing to the top was now gone. Ever since that meeting in his office, every time they met or talked, it was all business, no more joking around, no more extras like the good old days when he would take off day trips in the corporate jet to St. John to relax.

In that off season, Yorkey unloaded a couple of pitchers and replaced them with minor league prospects. The team had lost Hector Vasquez, their number one pitcher to free agency too, when Yorkey would not match Baltimore's offer.

Spring training felt different. Bob Startlin was hard to talk to and Hanratty was never around the cage like he had been before. The season started badly, but the team rallied just before the all star break and was in first place from mid August on. Despite losing key players, the team managed to finish on top of the Central and some hot bats, led by Brad, carried the team to another World Series title in 6 games against the Giants. But still, the clubhouse camaraderie and looseness was gone. Brad had another stellar year, hitting .327 but was physically and mentally exhausted by the end of the World Series. He had met Marisa during the season. She was a cheerleader for the Detroit Pride, the Lions cheerleading squad. They had been randomly paired at a charity golf outing and immediately hit it off. After a few dates, she moved in with him in mid August. Brad found himself thinking more about her than hitting the ball. He dreaded leaving town for road trips and called her twice a day while he was gone. In spite of this distraction, he had some of his most productive road trips in his career. He hit .509 with 11 homers and 19 runs batted in during one memorable

15 game road trip and was named player of the week for two consecutive weeks. Somehow, it didn't mean as much to him because she was not there to witness it. She had watched every game on television and told him how studly he looked on television, but still he longed to be home. At last in her arms after one of the team's roadtrips, he asked her to marry him. She had immediately said yes and they started to plan for the wedding. Three weeks later he pulled a hamstring and went on the DL for the second time in his career. This time, he didn't work hard during rehabilitation, and when his hamstring healed, he was out of shape.

"Screw it", he told her one night after she asked why he had not worked out, "I don't need to work that hard. My body and mind know what to do once I get back out there."

"You're not a young guy anymore, baby, your body needs time to heal and you need to keep sharp by staying in shape. I'd hate to see you get sent to Toledo," she said as she poked his side.

"Ha ha, funny girl. I know it, and they know it, that even sitting on this couch, I'm the best player they've got. Correction, that they've ever had! When my hamstring is ready, I'll go back out there and show them like I always do."

The hamstring healed, Brad did not show them. He struggled upon his return and had the worst September of his career as the Tigers missed the playoffs again. After the season, Brad had a series of tests done on the hamstring, and although it had healed, he still felt a tinge of pain when he walked and it was worse when he tried to run. He rested it as much as he could that fall before beginning off-season workouts in December. He was working himself back into shape, but still felt tightness when he pushed his workout too far.

This concerned him, and not wanting to injure the leg any further, did not push himself to top fitness.

He was sluggish in Florida and came out of spring training less than confident his hamstring would hold up. But the season had gone fairly well. He was tested a few times, and the leg held up. He was just starting to get full confidence when Rodriquez slammed into his leg and tore his quad.

Now here he was, running effortlessly at 15 miles per hour, not breathing hard, hardly even sweating. The pain and injuries of the past year and a half faded from his memory with each stride. Could he really be getting stronger than he'd ever been with these little miracle workers in his body rebuilding what time had slowly broken down? Could he return better than ever? Better than anyone ever? What about the repairs they were making on his good leg? A bonus! A frickin bonus. He and Barry were going to clean up for sure and show Yorkey what he is still capable of. Show him what a bad move it was to shop him? Show him for giving up on him.

"How much time now Alice?"

"One hour and ten minutes, Brad. You're vitals have not changed since two minutes in."

"Then you can go ahead and say I'm invincible," he said, hopping off the treadmill. "I don't think I need to show you anymore today." He grabbed a towel, wiped his barely wet face, snapped it at her playfully and turned and left the room.

Waiting until she no longer heard his footsteps, she picked up the phone and dialed.

Chapter 22

"Dr. Gupta, Alice here, he just left. No he did not max out. One hour and ten minutes. No, it stayed at 115 the whole time. Oh much longer, I'm sure. Probably all day."

On his way back to his room, Brad popped into the control room as was now his habit. He walked straight over to the topo and smiled at the green dots which were scattered all over the body on the screen. Blue ones were in motion everywhere and the red directors were still cluelessly gathered around the left knee. He glanced over at the counter screen. 160 directors were still active. Taking a deep breath and exhaling slowly, he looked at Joe the technician and said, "What a beautiful day it is, eh Joe?"

After the call from Alice, Dr. Gupta had called Dr. Childress and told him to gather the team and meet in his office.

When the team had gathered, Dr. Gupta rose from his desk, walked to his white board, grabbed a marker and drew a crude outline of a human body. As he spoke he made circles on the body at both biceps, around the chest and at the forearms.

"Gentleman and ladies, we have proven that our process can work in a human body. We, or I should say, the bots, have done in one week what it would take nature 6 months or more to achieve. This, as you know, as we have all worked hard to achieve, opens up many possibilities for the human race. We can seriously think now about healing any human ailment, restoring that which has been broken, that which has been weakened by the ravages of time and toil. We can now speak of mankind as a species in charge of its own destiny. The work we are doing now will be looked upon as the first step in achieving human immortality. For that we can all be proud of the work and effort we have put forth at the Institute.

But first, we have a bit of a problem to solve. Our subject as you know has been making remarkable progress, in fact, too remarkable. It seems the builders have not entered their shutdown routine. The primary objective was achieved, however, and we do not at this time understand it, but the directors were unable to issue the commands for the builders to stop and proceed to the evacuation area for discharge. Instead, the builders appear to have, on their own, begun to explore his body looking for more work. They have succeeded by repairing an otherwise nearly healthy quad on the subject's right leg. Attempts to communicate with the directors thus far have failed. For some unknown reason, we have an alarming number of director bots shutting down and/or failing to communicate either with us or the builders. It also appears the builders are somehow directing the miners to continue to search for, mine, and transport raw materials to the new repair sites. Tests indicate the quad on the right side is now at 100% as well as the injured left quad. These developments are concerning and at the same time, most pleasing. Dr. Childress, would you like to speak of the technical dilemma we now face?"

"As Dr. Gupta stated", Dr. Childress began, "it appears our programming has a bug. The directors had been instructed to shut the operation down when the quad on the left leg reached the 100%

mass target. What we think happened instead was this: as the building approached completion, some builders and all the miners were left with nothing to do. Instead of defaulting on their own to the evacuation, the idle builders went looking for more to do. When they encountered damage due to aging, not injury, in the right quad, they set about fixing it. The miners were instructed by the now reactivated builders to bring raw materials to the new work site. All of the bots involved in the new project severed communication with the directors because the directors were still only aware of the original mission, and therefore had neither control nor commands to direct the freed builders and miners to obey. Thinking the bots had abandoned the work site for evacuation; the directors went to 'end of job' and ceased to function. We theorize this is the case by the steady drop in active director bots. Soon, perhaps within three days, all directors will become inactive. What will happen at that time? We don't know. We theorize there will be no noticeable change since the builders have already shown an ability to direct their own actions and those of the miners. In the meantime, we have noticed a further migration to other parts of Mr. Dickson's body as Dr. Gupta has shown here and here", Dr. Childress said, pointing to the biceps on the screen. "We fear the builders are again in search of more work as the new project nears completion.

If left unchecked, I'm afraid Mr. Dickson's bots will continue to repair and improve his muscles indefinitely. If this were to happen, the increased muscle mass, although desirable at first, could lead to gross enlargement of all his muscle groups, causing increased workload for his heart and perhaps ultimately lead to heart failure."

"But don't you think his heart muscle will also benefit from bot repair?" one of the researcher's asked.

"Good point, but that remains to be seen. The heart muscle is different from the structural muscles in many ways. The builders may not recognize it as a muscle, or even worse, instigate repair using the wrong materials, causing muscle deformation, and perhaps catastrophic failure.

As tempting as it is to allow the project to run its course and see how much total improvement can be achieved, I'm afraid we must stop the builders and cease the repairs."

"Don't you think Brad needs to make that decision? After all, he's the one who offered his body for this advancement?" Joe asked.

"We will give Mr. Dickson the opportunity to understand the situation before we kill the remaining bots, but do it we must", Dr. Gupta interjected. "We cannot let him leave this building with active bots in his body. We have no idea what that outcome would be and we cannot have the company involved in any adverse situation. I will talk to him in the morning and we will perform the procedure in the afternoon. Dr. Childress, have your team prepare the radiation protocol, to be ready by noon tomorrow."

Chapter 23

Brad was reading the latest Sports Illustrated article speculating about the Twins chances of capturing the Central, now that Brad was out for the season, when there was a light rap on his door.

"Come in, it's unlocked."

Brad looked up as the door opened and Alice quickly stepped inside and closed the door behind her.

"I knew you loved me too, but you do know I'm engaged to be married?" Brad also added, "Maybe a quickie wouldn't hurt though."

"Very funny, but I'm not here for that and I don't have much time and I really shouldn't be here, but there's something you need to know."

Alice's sudden lack of humor got his attention.

"There was a meeting today after your marathon treadmill workout. Dr. Gupta called the entire team together and announced he was pulling the plug."

"Pulling the plug? On me?"

"Yes, on you. As you may have suspected something has gone wrong, very wrong. The team has lost control of the bots. The builders are repairing muscle in your body they were not supposed to repair. The team is worried the nanos will continue to repair muscle in your body until your heart can't take it anymore and it will stop. Dr. Gupta does not think it would be good for the Institute if that were to happen. He's afraid the word will get out and the government or AMA or both will move to shut him down. He does not want the project to go on any longer and has ordered the radiation protocol."

"The what?"

"Brad, you were never told about it because Dr. Gupta was sure he would be able to control the bots. But he has lost control. They've tried everything to get control back and all attempts have failed. The radiation protocol is a process where a high dosage of radiation, think 100 plus X-rays, would be applied to your body and cause all the bots to cease to function. Instead of going to the evacuation area, they would just be absorbed into your body and hopefully, be removed by natural cleansing."

"Hopefully? What if I don't want the bots killed? I rather like the progress they are making. I feel healthier and stronger than I have ever felt in my life."

"I'm afraid you have no choice. Dr. Gupta has decided it is more important to protect the reputation of the Institute than to see what may happen in the natural course."

"I will refuse to let them do it. I'll just leave. Tonight."

"You can't. He's ordered a shutdown of the building. No one gets in or out until the protocol is run and the results are known."

"When do they plan to run the protocol?"

"He plans to discuss your options with you tomorrow morning, after our PT. The thing is, he will tell you there are options, but the only option you will be given is the option to agree. If you don't, they plan to gas your room when you return to shower. And apply the treatment while you are out."

They can't do it. I will refuse and walk out the door."

"You are trapped Brad. They will not let you leave this place with live bots."

"Why are you telling me this? Why do you want me to know this?"

"I've watched you these past few days. You are an amazing person. Today during your endurance test, I was told to run you to the absolute limit of human endurance. Instead you got there easily and then surpassed that. The look on your face was pure joy and achievement. It was incredible watching you. I think there is more potential. I think you could become the strongest human ever to live. Just think of what could eventually happen. Every single muscle in your body, all 639 of them, built to perfection. All of them functioning at optimum level. Just imagine what you could do on the field, in life. I just hate to see that opportunity taken from you. You deserve to make your own choice."

Brad rose from his chair. He walked to the mirror. Every single muscle tuned to perfection? He could do anything; he could reach heights he'd only dreamed of before. He could play ball forever. Most of all, he could insure the Tigers would win the Series and he would make a fortune on the bet.

"I choose not to stop the bots. But how can I get out of here?"

"Leave that to me," She said, squeezed his arm affectionately, and quietly left the room.

Bard flexed his muscles in front of the mirror, followed by a 'Hulk" pose and flopped down on the bed. It looked to be a long night.

Chapter 24

Bill, the night security guard, saw Alice walking up the sidewalk at 3 AM. In her arms, a box, about 1 foot square. It was not unusual to see a researcher or technician at this hour, but he couldn't recall ever seeing Alice this late. He leaned forward on the control panel and pushed the intercom button, "Evening, Ms. Perkins, what brings you here at this hour?"

"Hey Bill. Dr. Gupta wanted me to summarize my work the past few days for Mr. Dickson's physical therapy. I just got it done and wanted to bring it over so it would be on his desk when he gets here in the morning."

"You do know we are on Code Yellow lockdown don't you?"

"Yes I was here yesterday when it was declared. I'll show you what's in the box, just papers."

"OK, come on through," he said, clicking the button that disarmed the magnetic release on the door. "You know I have to check it anyway."

Alice walked through the double doors, glancing up at the security camera mounted between them. She gave it a little smile and walked through.

"Everyone's pretty skittish tonight," he said as she placed the box on the check-in table. He lifted the top off and peered inside. In it were a couple of manila folders and papers. He absently thumbed through one of the folders, papers full of graphs and numbers. He had no idea what he was looking at. At length, he looked up at Alice and said, "More people here than I've ever seen."

"Oh really," she said trying to hide her surprise. "Who's here?"

"A couple of the researchers, Fred and Stan, four of the technicians, including that new gal, and Dr. Childress. All came in about 11 or so. Been back there ever since, haven't seen one of them."

"Where are they, do you know?"

Tony looked at his video displays. "They're all in the control room, see?"

Alice leaned over the table and looked at the screen Bill was pointing to. The group of eight were gathered by the topo station and involved in what appeared to be an animated conversation. Dr. Childress was pointing at the screen and was talking. It appeared he was trying to make a point or give instructions, because with the other hand, he was gesturing wildly.

Alice glanced briefly around the panel at the other screens which showed no signs of life in the physical therapy room, hallways or labs. Good she thought.

"I'm just going to go put these in Dr. Gupta's office and check some things in my PT room. Shouldn't be too long."

"I'm sorry, Dr. Gupta's office is locked and off limits tonight, that order came from the boss himself."

"Then I'll just put them on his secretary's desk," she said, wheels already spinning in her head to come up quickly with a plan B.

"That would be ok. How long do you think you'll be back there?"

"It shouldn't take me more than a few minutes, I'll just drop this box off then I need to do a few things in my PT room. I'll be back soon. I'm tired and want to get back home and go to bed. Big day tomorrow."

"That's what everyone's been saying, see you in a few."

With that, Bill sat back down, watched Alice open and disappear through Dr. Gupta's outer office door, then returned his attention to the book he had been reading.

Alice flicked on the light and looked around the room. She was always a bit surprised by the sparse furnishings in this room. She walked over to Dr. Gupta's office door and grabbed the knob. Indeed it was locked. She then walked over to his receptionist's desk and placed the box on it. She opened the lid, lifted the folders and drew out a bag that had been concealed beneath them. She grabbed a pen from the desk and wrote on the box:

"Brad Dickson Physical Therapy Eval"

Alice threw the pen back on the desk and left the room.

On her walk down the hall, she could hear voices in the control room. She wished she could understand what they were saying but it was too muffled to make out. She distinctly heard Dr. Childress; his voiced raised, but still could not make out what he was saying. She dared not linger for fear someone might leave the control room and discover her in the hall.

She continued to her physical therapy lab. As always, she inhaled deeply through her nose when she opened the door. The smell of sweat always permeated the room and it was a smell she had grown to anticipate and love. She flicked on the light and pulled

136

out her cell phone. After quickly browsing her address book, she tapped the phone's face.

After only two rings a familiar voice answered, "Hello."

"Brad, its Alice. I got your cell phone number from your patient information sheet. I've come to help you get out of here."

"Where are you and how are you going to get me out of here?"

"We don't have much time so listen carefully. I'm in the PT room now. There is a bag on my desk. Inside of the bag, there is a technician's smock and a wig. I am going to distract the guard in a few minutes. When I do, you need to go to the PT room, put on the smock and wig and go to the receiving door in the back. To get there, when you leave the PT room, make a left, go to the end of the hall, make a right and then go through the research lab door; which is halfway down that hall on the left. At the rear of the lab is a door that says RECEIVING above it. Push the door release button and go through the door. You will be in the loading dock area. Go down the stairs to the right of the dock. Next to the right-most overhead door is a walk-in door. Push the release door button there and you will be outside the building. Go down the alley to the next building and come around to the other side of that building and wait. In a few minutes I will leave. When I do, I will drive your way and as I slow down, you will need to run out to my car and jump in. We only have a few minutes, so you will need to move fast. Got all of that?"

"Yes, Alice, go through the lab to the loading dock, I think I have it. I can't thank you enough for helping me."

"I sure hope this works, because we could both be in serious trouble if we get caught," she said, a hint of fear in her voice. "OK, give me 5 minutes from right now, then get going. See you in a few."

Brad looked at the time on his phone, 3:14. "Got it, 5 minutes."

Alice shut off her light and walked back to the security desk. Bill put down his book as she approached. "Got 'er done, eh, Ms. Perkins?"

"Yep. Just wanted to clean up some equipment I forgot to do today. I thought as long as I was here, might as well get things ready for tomorrow. Say, Bill, let me ask you a question."

"I dunno, I'm pretty busy here,", he said with a laugh, holding his arms out to show her his empty world. "But I think I can spare a few minutes for a purdy lady."

She smiled at his flirtatious reply, "I've noticed you are well built, and I've meant to ask but never seemed to have the time, but I'm curious, how long did it take you to develop your muscular build, if you don't mind me asking?"

"Heck no, Ms. Perkins.

"Please, Bill, call me Alice."

"Heck no, Alice," he drawled her name out as if saying the word for the first time in his life. "My dad was a football player, played for the Boilermakers in college for two years until he hurt his back. Anyway, he started me early. I can remember throwing a football with him when I was 3 years old, honest, I do remember it, in our back yard. We did that most every day. I can remember times he

138

would come home and we'd play until it got dark. Mom got so mad at him for keeping me out, but we had a great time. As I got older, my first organized ball was in Little All-American football in middle school. I was kind of a big kid, so they always had me play a lineman, offense and defense. Dad made sure I stayed in shape and I think it was about 8th grade, he brought home a weight bench set. I had to work out on that bench 3 times during the week and Saturday. Mom wouldn't let me work out on Sundays. But when she'd go shopping or visiting, I'd sneak down stairs and do a few sets."

While Bill talked, Alice glanced up at the monitor board and saw Brad leave his room and slip into the PT room. She then returned her attention to Bill's story.

"I really liked football, and I loved to knock people down. After ninth grade, during that summer, I mean, I got to go to a football camp. It was put on by the Northwestern coaching staff. It was an intense week. We worked hard in the hot sun all day. Scrimmage after scrimmage, all day long. The coaches taught us cool stuff about blocking and tackling. We ran, ran a lot. Did the obstacle course twice a day, and exercised all the time. I can't remember how many times I puked, I mean, got sick, sorry. Every morning and night we would hit the weight room. Being one of the bigger kids, I was teased about my size and everyone thought I should be able to lift more than anyone else, which I did."

Alice caught the image of Brad, in his white coat; disappear into the lab as Bill droned on.

"It was at that camp, I changed. Working out somehow quit being work and started being fun. I couldn't wait to get into the weight room to improve what I had done the day before. I came out of that camp a different kid."

Brad opened the lab door and quickly closed it behind him. The lab coat was a little snug, and the arms too short, but it would do. He had trouble fitting the black wig on his head, and it tilted a little to the side, but he got it to snug on and hoped it wouldn't pop off. He walked quickly through the lab between cages. Some of the larger animals stirred when he entered the room and a couple of the birds made squawking noise when their sleep was interrupted. The lighting was dim as the room was lit only by every other row of fluorescents, so Brad had a hard time seeing into the cages, but about halfway down the hall, the animal in one cage caught his attention. He stopped and peered into the cage. The creature in it was a rat, he was sure, because it had the pointed nose of a rat and a long tail. But the body was grotesquely deformed. The shoulders on each side formed two humps, nearly twice the side of its head. The back legs stuck straight out and were as big around as the rat's torso. The rat's front legs also stuck straight out and looked like cones, with the wide part near its torso, scaling down to a point just above the feet. It was lying on its side and the torso jutted out in six places, looking like it had swallowed a six pack of beer bottles. Brad looked on the label at the top of the cage, it read: "Skeletal Muscle 6-14-2025". Brad looked closely because he noticed movement. The tips of the six bumps on the torso were indeed in motion. Each mound flickered in a haphazard fashion.

Brad didn't linger, he had to get to the loading dock. As he ran, he noticed other cages with more deformed rats. The cages had labels of "Smooth Muscle", "Ligament", and "Bone Marrow". An empty cage on the end said "Cardiac Muscle 9-12-2025 Terminated".

He reached the door and pressed the button. He heard the magnet release. At the same time, a light on the control panel board lit up. Bill stopped talking and looked at the screen for the lab. "Fred really needs to quit smoking," he said and returned to his story as Brad slipped through the door. A moment later, Brad pressed the final button and disappeared into the alley. Bill didn't even look up this time as he knew where the technicians smoked behind the building.

"So by high school," Bill was deep into his teen years, "I was benching 450 pounds and….."

"Sorry Bill, but I just remembered I left a pizza in the oven at home. I'm afraid I have to leave. I do want to hear the rest of your story and schedule you for endurance testing, but right now I'm afraid I have to get going."

"I can come in any time you want, Ms. Perkins. I only live a few blocks away. I'd be happy to help your research."

"Thank you, I will get with you later this week." With that she hurried out the door. Bill watched her until her car pulled away from the curb. He looked up at the video board, and thought to himself, "Dang, that was a quick smoke," as he counted the eight people in the control room.

Alice slowed and Brad ran from the side of the building and hopped in. "I owe you big time sweetheart," he said, removing the wig and lab coat.

Chapter 25

"Oh baby, it's so good to see you. I was worried sick when the Institute called this morning and said you had left unexpectedly during the night." Marisa ran to the door and threw her arms around him as he came through, "What happened?"

"The Institute called? When?"

"It was just after 8. I was eating and the phone rang. That nice Dr. Gupta said you had left and wondered if I had seen you yet."

"What did you tell him?"

"Of course, I told him no, I didn't expect you for another day."

"Then what did he say?"

"He said when I do see you to please call him so he would know where you were, and that you made it home safely. He sounded upset like he was in a hurry. What happened babe?"

"Nothing happened. They were going to terminate me today anyway, because I had made better progress that they had hoped. I missed you so much, so I just decided to check out last night and come home to be with you. Honey, I'm completely healed, look at my leg." He rolled his pant leg up and showed her the bulging muscle he had developed. "Not only that, but look at the right leg." He rolled that pant leg up and she saw an equally enlarged thigh muscle.

"Great Brad," then hesitantly added, "weren't they only going to fix your ripped quad?"

"Yes, this may sound bizarre, but when the robots fixed my left quad, they went looking for more work and decided to repair the right one as well. In fact, right now as we speak, the little guys are still in there fixing up my whole body. Every single muscle will be fixed, just like before, hell, better than they've ever been. I'll be stronger and faster than nature had ever intended. I'll be able to play ball for years."

A frown formed on her face, "That's wonderful babe, but weren't the nanos supposed to fix your left quad and then exit your body. I mean, wasn't that what they were programmed to do?"

"Yes, in a way. They were programmed to build muscle. During the process they discovered other muscles in my body that needed repair too, so they just went about the job they were designed to do, fix muscle. Don't worry, when they are done, they will exit, just like they are supposed to do."

"But what if they don't? What if they stay active and keep making muscle tissue, what's going to happen then?" Marisa was starting to grasp the situation.

"Honey, relax. That can't happen. The Institute told me there is absolutely no chance. The bots only have a lifespan of three weeks, so no matter where they are in the process they will cease to function and die. My body will absorb them and eventually flush them out naturally. Not to worry."

"Are you going to call Dr. Gupta now?"

"No, I will in a bit, but first, I need to go see Mr. Yorkey and see the surprise on that tightwad's face when he sees me. If the

Institute calls again before I get a chance to call Dr. Gupta, tell them you haven't seen me yet, OK?"

"OK."

Brad quickly showered and headed out to Comerica Park. Yorkey's going to wet himself he thought, as a big wide grin grew on his face.

Chapter 26

"Mr. Dickson has left us and the Institute in a very dangerous position. I want him found now!" Dr. Gupta was addressing Dr. Childress and Steve Morris, the head of security for Gupta Institute, who had gathered in his office.

When the guard went in to get Brad at 7 AM and discovered the room empty, all hell broke loose. A thorough search of the building failed to turn him up. When they reviewed the video replay on the security cameras, they saw where he had snuck out of his room, gone into the PT room, donned a technicians smock and walked out of the building through the loading dock. The night guard, Bill, was adamant the surveillance system must have malfunctioned, because he had monitored the system continuously during his entire shift, like always.

"Attempts to locate him thus far have not been successful. We must find him and disable the nanobots, but we must be very discreet. Word of this could ruin the Institute."

"We are pretty sure it was Mr. Dickson who rented a car from Enterprise at 4:37 this morning at O'Hare," Morris spoke up, "the man paid cash and said his name was Jones, but the description the attendant gave me sounded like him. He had been dropped off by a female driving a light colored small car. The same type and color of car Alice owns. Phone calls to Alice Perkins' home have gone unanswered and messages have not been returned. He rented the car for two days and paid cash. He did not have the GPS activated, so there is no way to know where the car is now. We suspect he has gone to Detroit. I have formulated a plan to take a team there and will be ready by this afternoon. We will transport a portable radiation machine as well. When we get our hands on him, we will dose him and that will be the end of it. His fiancé claims she hasn't seen him, but I suspect she is lying. He would have had plenty of time to drive there. Our plan will be to stake out his home and intercept him there."

"Gentlemen," Dr. Gupta rose as he spoke, "we cannot fail."

An urgent rap on the door interrupted their discussion. Dr. Gupta's secretary peeked in, "Sorry to barge in doctor, but you might want to turn on your TV to ESPN. It's Mr. Dickson, sir."

Chapter 27

Alice Perkins was nervous. She had not gone home after helping Brad get to the car rental agency. The Institute kept ringing her cellphone and leaving messages, but she did not answer. She drove around the city for a few hours; afraid to stop anywhere someone might see her. Finally, exhausted from being up all night, she determined it was probably ok since the calls from the Institute had stopped. Perhaps they had given up trying to reach her.

She pulled the car slowly into the attached garage. Wearily, she got out of her car and pushed the button to close the overhead door as she inserted her house key into the lock. She walked into the kitchen and threw the keys on the counter. What a night! She was exhausted and really needed a beer. She reached in the fridge and as she shut the door, she saw Steve Morris standing next to the refrigerator. She shrieked and started to run, but Steve had already reached out and grabbed her arm, hard. She dropped the beer on the floor and he spun her around and threw her against the wall. She lunged out at him, but he dodged her advance and grabbed a clump of hair on the back of her head, and threw her against the wall again. Her legs buckled and she slid down the wall. She would have sat on the floor had Steve let her. He lifted her by the clump of hair he still had in his hand and led her to the living room where he threw her on the couch.

"Where is he?"

"Where's who," she replied, getting a smack across her face for the effort.

147

"You know who. Where is he?"

"I'm afraid I don't know who you mean."

"So that's how you want to play, eh? You know who I mean, Brad Dickson."

"Why do you think I know where Brad is?"

"Don't play innocent with me. What were you doing at the Institute at 3 AM?"

As coolly as she could muster, "I was delivering some reports that Dr. Gupta wanted me to finish. I just wanted to make sure they were there when he got there in the morning."

"Delivering reports, eh? Not bringing clothes for Mr. Dickson?"

"That's right, reports for Dr. Gupta. Ask him."

"And you were not distracting Bill while Mr. Dickson made his escape?"

"No, I remember talking to Bill about doing some tests."

"And you did not drive Mr. Dickson to the car rental later?"

Alice did not have an answer for that one. How did they know? How had they learned so fast? Why were they so worried about Brad getting away?

"Steve," she pleaded, "they were going to destroy him. Do you understand they were going to irradiate him and poison him, and make it look like an accident? I had to do something. I had to help him."

Steve got to his feet. He reached over and grabbed her hard by the arm, "you shouldn't have," and lifted her from the couch and walked toward the door, with Alice in tow.

"Where are you taking me?"

"To go swimming in Lake Michigan, with Bill."

Chapter 28

As Brad exited the freeway, he was getting excited to see the look on Yorkey's face when he bounced into his office, healed and ready to play. Yorkey will have a cow, he thought. He pulled the car into the player's lot and hopped out, sprinting up to the stadium. Very few people were around, which is usually the case when the team is on the road. They were in the middle of their last road trip, barely hanging on to first place over the surging Sox. Brad slipped his card through the security reader and briskly walked to the elevator.

"Hi Claudia," Brad announced to Yorkey's longtime assistant and he bridged the gap to his private office. "Big guy in?"

Before Claudia had a chance to speak or stop him, Brad grabbed the knob and entered Al Yorkey's private office.

The walls were lined with pictures of teams and players from all of the Detroit Tigers' glorious past. Autographed pictures of many of the greats lined all four walls. Al Kaline, Hank Greenburg, and Willie Horton among them and the crown jewel, a rare picture of Ty Cobb. A recent picture of Justin Verlander at his Hall of Fame induction occupied the wall just behind Yorkey. A picture of Brad receiving his first MVP trophy used to hang there, but now Brad didn't see it, as he scanned the room.

"Hi Al, what's up?" Brad calmly said to an obviously surprised Al Yorkey, who jumped when the door burst open. "Ready for the playoffs?"

Al Yorkey was a calm man, calm when negotiating with agents, calm when talking to reporters, calm when playing poker, but he was not calm at this moment. He dropped the pen he was holding and for a long moment could not speak. He looked down at Brad's leg, then back to Brad's smiling face, and finally after a long pause of silence and in a shaky voice said, "Brad, how wonderful to see you. When did you get back?"

"Surprised to see me Al? Look at this leg, completely healed." Brad hopped around the room like a sugar-dosed 5 year-old. "I'm ready for the playoffs."

"But, Brad, how in the world? I mean, what did you do? I mean Doc Lewis told me you were definitely done for the year. No chance whatsoever, with maybe six months rehab after surgery?"

"Well sawbones Lewis doesn't know everything does he, Al?" Brad was enjoying this form of torture. "I found a way to help my team this year, and I'm going to do it. You do want me to help the team this year, don't you Al?"

"Of course I do, Brad. I just thought you were done and we were going to try our best without you."

"You don't have to worry about that now, Al. You can send Gutierrez back home for the winter. I plan to suit up for the playoffs. No, not just ready, I plan to be at 110% for the playoffs. You see, I don't quit. I don't give up on my friends. I don't give up on my team. I find a way to do my job, regardless if others have given up on me or not. I am going to show them, you, that I'm as good as ever. I'm going to have a great postseason. No, I'm going to have the greatest postseason you've ever seen. People are going to be sorry they gave up on Brad Dickson."

He did not give Yorkey time to reply, for he spun around and sprinted to the door. "Make room for another trophy, Al." And he was gone.

Yorkey, still rattled, picked up his phone, "Claudia, have Hanratty come to my office." He hung up the phone and buried his head in his hands.

Back in his car, Brad pulled out his cellphone and dialed his agent, "Barry, call your guy at ESPN and tell him I'm back and will be ready for the playoffs.

"Brad, you're back? You're in Detroit? What's going on?"

"I just spoke with Yorkey and he's overcome with joy that I'm ready to play. I just left his office and he is speechless."

"That's great news, Brad. How is the leg?"

"You won't believe it. The leg feels better than ever. My right leg's better too. I ran for 2 hours yesterday and didn't even work up a sweat."

"But how?"

"I'll tell you all about it later, but now you need to get the news on the air that I'm back. Also, everything's square with Tony, right?"

"Yes, we put the bets down day before yesterday, completely legit, in Tony's name. The odds for the Tigers went to 50 to 1 the day after you got hurt. We covered $2 million across three houses."

"Pretty good wages for one little hit," Brad said singsong to the tune of the Jesus Christ Superstar song as he hung up.

Dr. Gupta turned up the volume as the ESPN newscaster spoke:

"And to repeat the top story, Detroit Tigers all-star third baseman, Brad Dickson, who suffered what appeared to be a season ending leg injury two weeks ago has now been cleared to rejoin the team for the Tigers playoff roster. Our source tells us the team doctor misdiagnosed the injury and Dickson went to an undisclosed clinic to have the knee examined. According to our sources, they found only temporary damage in the knee and through an intense rehabilitation and supplement program; they were able to repair the damage. It is unknown at this time where Dickson went, but it sure sounds like a miracle, doesn't it Brian?"

Dr. Gupta stroked his beard, "This complicates things."

Chapter 29

Word quickly spread through the team's hotel as the Tigers' staff and players lounged around waiting for the last game of the road trip against the Rays. Bob Startlin was pleased and surprise to hear his third baseman would be ready to go when they entered the playoffs. He had a tough year dealing with the injuries. But that was just part of the deal. At 67 years of age, he had given a lot of thought during the season about calling it quits. He wanted more time with his grandkids, which now numbered 7; with another due any day. He wanted to enjoy his ranch in the summer time, fish at the nearby stream, enjoy his retirement. A lifetime of major league baseball had robbed him of every summer for as long as he could remember. He had purchased the ranch nearly 15 years ago and promised Jojo, his bride of 43 years, he would manage three more years, or until he got fired and then they could enjoy their golden years together. Having the kids and grandkids out to the ranch, travel together and see places they've read and talked about over the years.

That all changed though when Al Yorkey came calling with a convincing story and a huge checkbook. "Come manage my team. We've got the number one pick and we are going to build a championship team around this Dickson kid. Bob, you are the only manager in the world who I want to take us to the top and keep us there. You will have the final decision on personnel, just tell Hanratty who you want or need and I'll make sure it's taken care of to your liking. You will have full support from me and the front office for all on-field decisions as well. We will stay out of your hair. If there are any problems with players, Don will handle it. I want you to focus on putting nine players out there that will bring titles to Detroit. Anything you want or need, I will provide. "

Al Yorkey lived up to that promise, at least for the first few years. He gave Bob complete control over the baseball on-field operation. When Bob would mention to Yorkey that he needed a left hand reliever, Yorkey went out and got Greg Yancey, the best available. When he needed another strong bat in the lineup, Yorkey spent $100 million on Perez on a long term deal. It was the dream job. Despite Jojo's stated disappointment, he knew she understood he was doing things he had only dreamed of at other stops he had made in his long managerial career. He was forming a dynasty and she couldn't take that away from him. Still, he felt guilty because he had broken the promise he had made to her so many years ago. They were not getting any younger and with her health problems worsening in recent years, they had all but given up on being able to travel and see the world as they had always talked about.

In recent years, as things started going sour for Oogle, Yorkey had become increasingly impatient with him. Even on a few occasions Yorkey had made suggestions of who needed to be in or out of the lineup. He no longer could get a player just by asking. Yorkey had told him more than once that he'd just have to make do with what he had and manage the team. Despite the tightening of the purse strings, Bob had been able to get the most out of his remaining stars and upcoming prospects. The fact he had won Manager of the Year award last season had less to do with player talent and more to do with his managerial skill. The baseball writers understood that when they voted him in. But it had crossed his mind many times this year that it was time to give it up. Yes, he had made up his mind, after Brad went down, whether the team made the post season or not, he would tell Yorkey he was done and retire to his ranch and his Jojo.

Sitting alone in his room, he reflected on the season, one with many challenges, especially the bad run of injuries. Every team has injuries, he reasoned, it's up to the skipper to put together a lineup that had the best chance of winning.

Before Brad went down, he had juggled five different players in the middle infield in the last two months, never getting comfortable with the mix of veterans or the two they brought up from Toledo at the start of September. He hadn't needed to worry about third base though. Although his future hall of famer had lost a step and some hand/eye coordination in the past couple of years, he was still better than just about every third baseman Startlin had ever coached or seen. In the two weeks since losing him, the team had a definite drop off in talent both in the field and at the plate with the younger Gutierrez. He couldn't wait to put Brad's name back on the lineup card.

A knock on his door, interrupted his thoughts, he strolled over and opened it. His hitting coach, Johnny Matson, was standing there with a big grin on his face.

"Hey skip, did you hear the news about Brad. Remarkable, don't you think?"

"Yeah, John, I heard. Makes your job easier, eh?"

"Hell, yeah! Doc really screwed up his diag, don't you think?"

156

"Doctor Lewis is one of the best sports doctors on the planet. I highly doubt he messed up the diagnosis on Brad."

"Then what do you think happened? One day Brad's done and two weeks later, he's ready to play. Something just ain't right somewhere. Am I right?"

"John, I'm not sure what to make of it. I will be anxious to talk to Brad though and find out the name of that witch doctor he went to. Maybe he can help Jojo."

"Mayhaps," Johnny offered, "whatever happened, I'm looking forward to getting home and getting ready for the playoffs."

"Let's win this one tonight first. We still have to clinch the division. And we know the Sox aren't going to just give it to us. Make sure you get BP going at 4 today. It's an early 6:30 game."

That night the Tigers seemed like a different team. Maybe it was a case of getting inspiration from the news of their star coming back, maybe the excitement of getting home to take on the hated Sox, maybe the anticipation of the post season. Whatever it was, the 8 to 0 spanking of the Rays felt good on the plane ride home.

Chapter 30

The next morning, Bob was in his office when the phone rang.

"Hello."

"May I speak to Mr. Startlin please?" An unfamiliar voice with a hint of a Mideastern accent, he thought.

"Speaking. And who am I speaking to?"

"Mr. Startlin, my name is Rasheesh Gupta. I am a doctor of nanobiotechnology and director of the Gupta Institute of Nano Robotics. I am calling you about one of your team members, a Mr. Brad Dickson. I was wondering sir if you have seen Mr. Dickson recently?"

"No I haven't, not since he went on the DL a couple of weeks ago, and why is that a concern of yours, Dr. Gupta?"

"Mr. Dickson has been a recent patient of mine and I have been trying to reach him, but he does not seem to answer his phone and no one can tell me where he is. I have some information of interest to him and I would like to speak to him soon."

"A patient of yours?"

"Did I say 'patient'? Please excuse me I misspoke; I meant to say I recently corresponded with him on a personal matter and have the information he requested. Do you know when you might see him next?"

"We have a game tonight, so I expect to see him in the clubhouse very soon. All the ballplayers are required to be in the clubhouse by 4 PM on game days. Brad is usually early. I'm sure I will see him in the next hour or so." Looking at his watch and seeing it was a quarter til noon, he suspected Brad would walk in any minute.

"Would you please tell Mr. Dickson when you see him that I would like for him to call at his earliest convenience? It is really in his best interest if I can deliver the information today. Could you please do that for me?"

"Sure Dr. Gupta. Does he have your number?"

"Yes, I am sure he knows how to reach me. Thank you very much Mr. Startlin."

Dr. Gupta hung up. Bob stared at his phone for a moment before returning it to the cradle. I wonder what that's all about, he thought as he started toward the player's locker room.

There, as he suspected, Brad was already changing into his warm-ups.

"Brad, you are a sight for sore eyes," Bob called out as he approached the slugger, seated on a bench.

Brad reached out his hand and shook Bob's. "Hey skip. I'm ready to go. I couldn't let you do this without me, could I?"

"How's the leg. Last time I saw you, it looked pretty bad."

"It wasn't as bad as Lewis thought, I guess. I had some treatment and waa-laa, I'm ready to go."

"Treatment, what kind of treatment? Where?"

"You know, normal stuff, ice, massages, rub downs. The leg really responded well."

159

"Yeah I can see that," Bob replied looking down at Brad's well-developed leg. "Looks like you should have tried that treatment a long time ago. Your leg, in fact both of your legs look stronger and bigger than I think I've ever seen them."

"It was pretty intense PT, skip," Brad said pulling his sweats up and covering his enlarged thighs. "I wish I'd have done it years ago."

Brad got up to end the conversation, the less said the better. But his manager stopped him, tugging at his arm, "Well I'm glad you are ready to go. By the way, I had a call from a friend of yours a few minutes ago. He says you had requested some information and he's having trouble finding you. A Dr. Gupta from a robot shop. What the hell's that all about Brad?"

"It's nothing skip, I was just curious about some research they were doing and thought I might invest in their company."

"He sounded like it was important enough to track you down through me. Better give him a call; he sounded like it was urgent."

"I will, in a bit. Thanks skip. You know, I have a feeling this is going to be our best run ever!"

And our last, Bob thought.

On the third ring, the voice answered, "Hello, this is Dr. Gupta."

"Hi doc, I hear you're looking for me."

"Yes Mr. Dickson, so glad to hear from you. We have unfinished business. You should not have left the Institute in such a hurry."

"I had to Doc, I heard I was going to get nuked in the morning and I don't like getting nuked in the morning."

"Mr. Dickson, whatever it was you heard or understood, you were not going to get nuked. We were merely going to insure the procedure you were undergoing came to a successful conclusion. By leaving the Institute before we could do that, you have put yourself in danger. Perhaps grave danger."

"Oh really, why is that? I don't think I'm in danger. In fact I think my future looks pretty bright. I can feel muscles all over my body getting stronger. I think your procedure has done wonders. You should be telling the world, like I intend to do when the season is over."

"We are very proud of the achievements we have been able to accomplish with you, Mr. Dickson, but I'm afraid you will not want to tell anyone about what has happened, at least not until we are able to examine you and stop the procedure."

"Really?"

"Yes, really. You see, what we have determined is the nanobots in your body have malfunctioned. They were supposed to stop and evacuate when the process was finished. But due to an oversight on our part, they continue to repair muscle all over your body. I am afraid there is no stopping the process until we are able to kill off the bots. The shutdown mechanism will not work. The bots will go on building up muscle until the end."

"The end, the end of what?"

"The end of your life I'm afraid. You see, at some point we conjecture the builders will eventually find their way to your heart muscle. They will recognize the basic chemical and DNA structures, but they will not understand that the heart muscle is different. We feel they will go about building that muscle up too. An enlarged heart muscle, a condition clinically called cardiomyopathy is not desirable at all. That is the definition actually of heart disease. They will make your heart so big it will no longer pump blood. This will cause heart failure and you will go into cardiac arrest and die. The only way to prevent that is to stop the process before it starts. We are not trying to harm you. Quite the opposite, we are trying to save your life. You have seen for yourself, the builders and miners are out of control and are now spread all over your body. I suspect you woke up this morning with bigger abdominals and pectorals than you had yesterday, am I correct? Soon they will find your heart."

"I don't believe you. I suspect you want to get me back to your lab, so you can remove any evidence of the nanobots before the FDA finds out you've been experimenting on humans with an experimental procedure. Don't worry; they will not get any cooperation from me. You have extended my career by many years, I will not rat you out, but I will not let you kill these miracle workers either. Not until they've maximized every muscle in my body."

"Mr. Dickson, you are endangering your life. You are in danger of shortening it, not the opposite. Please let us remove the nanobots before they destroy you."

"No thanks, I like me just how I am." And with that, he poked the phone "end" button to disconnect the call.

He walked to the mirror, and flexing his muscles was pleased with how his chest popped out. No one's going to take this away from me, no one.

That night in his miraculous return from the DL, Brad had three home runs and helped the Tigers to an 11-3 rout of the second place Sox, clinching the Central title.

After the game, reporters gathered around his locker as usual, but this time it was more than the normal local guys. A reporter from ESPN and another from CNN were there to hear about his stellar night

"So Brad," the CNN reporter started out, shoving a microphone under Brad's nose, nearly hitting him. "We've heard you disappeared to get a mysterious treatment, and when you came back you were stronger than you've ever been. Can you tell us more about this treatment?"

"Haha, guys, there is no mysterious treatment. My body has always recovered fast from injuries. I just found a facility that worked with me to maximize my recovery and that's all there is to it. Sorry, no voodoo. Besides, my muscle injury was not as bad as it had been reported."

After finishing off the Sox two days later with a three game sweep, later that night, in bed, Maria put her arm around his chest, as she had done many times before. She was shocked at how large his pecs were. She could barely reach around his upper torso. The definition of his chest muscles was alarming to her.

"Brad, do you know how big your chest is getting?"

"Yes I do, isn't it wonderful?"

"No, it's scary."

"It is part of the treatment they did at the Institute."

"Do they know about this," she said, rubbing her hand across Brad's broad chest.

"Of course they know. They monitor everything that is happening to me," Brad tried to convince her. "It's just part of the program, hon. Really. Nothing to worry about. When the bots got done with the knee, they just went looking for more repairs to make, that's all. It's all really for the better good. When they are done making the repairs, they will go away. Don't worry. It's all under control."

He involuntarily flexed his chest muscles. They were getting big, bigger than even in his younger days, bigger than he could ever imagine. His arms too! He could feel every muscle in his chest and in his arms tight, straining against the skin.

He had a sudden itch on his cheek and reached up to scratch it. He rubbed a few times but it persisted. Nerves, he thought. It must be nerves. The ALDS will start in two days against the Angels and they are going to be tough. He rubbed a few more times, temporarily easing the itching sensation then laid back down on his back, hands behind his head, staring up at the black unseen ceiling, occasionally twitching his nose to relieve the itching in his face.

It was the worst night of sleep in his life he thought, as he rolled over and saw it was only 4:30 in the morning. I've never been nervous like this before a playoff series, what's the big deal? With my new body, I'll tear those Angels up. I'll beat them single-handedly. I just wish this itching would stop on my face. He unconsciously rubbed his cheek. It felt swollen. Probably from scratching so hard all night.

Marisa rolled in her sleep away from him. He waited a few moments for her to return to dreamland, and then he climbed out of bed. He went into the bathroom and turned the light on and leaned toward the mirror. His face was definitely puffy, both cheeks.

He opened the medicine cabinet, looked around on the shelves within, then started going through the vanity drawers; He finally pulled out a bottle of Skin So Soft and put a dollop in his hand. This always works on bug bites, he thought, maybe it will help with my nervous hives.

He rubbed the lotion all over his face then went back to bed.

Chapter 31

This was it, the biggest stage. Brad and the Tigers had dispatched the Angels easily and again humbled the White Sox. Now the only team that stood in the way of another World Series crown was the Cardinals. The Cards had an easy NLDS, sweeping the Giants, but just concluded a tough series with the Reds, finally beating them in the seventh game with a sacrifice fly in the bottom of the 11th by George Morris, their little used backup catcher. Now it was on to the Tigers and the hot Brad Dickson. Brad had hit .426 in the ALDS with 4 homers, and backed that up with a .468 in the ALCS, despite the White Sox reluctance to pitch to him. To go along with 7 intentional walks, he still managed to hit 4 home runs and drove in 12 runs.

But the articles and blog posts were not so much about his phenomenal series, but his larger physical size and newly rediscovered power.

Brad had been very quiet about the procedure. He was not available for any post-game interviews and was intentionally vague when an occasionally lucky reporter cornered him. He stuck to the story that his injury had not been as severe as originally reported and he used aggressive rehabilitation to get back into playing shape for the playoffs. He shrugged off suggestions that steroid use had contributed to his new and growing size.

"Working out, fellas, you oughtta try it someday," was his stock answer when asked about his increased bulk. If they continued to press, he would walk away from the interview.

Despite having a couple of good series, Brad thought his nerves should have settled down once the post season got under way, but the hives on his face continued to itch and give him problems. Skin so Soft was no longer working and he had Al obtain prescription Prednisone, to keep his histamines from going crazy. Prednisone proved little more effective than the lotion.

The swelling of his face was getting worse too. Every time he looked into the mirror, he was sure the size of his face had grown since the last time. He had large bloated cheeks, not just the kind of puffiness that is the result of a night spent drinking too much beer, but much more. Much fatter, and the skin was not loose and hanging under his eyes. It was taut and stretched almost smooth across his swollen, lumpy cheeks. It felt firm, tough. He would squish his face into a big broad grin and it felt like his cheeks would explode. That wasn't the only facial feature that had changed. His forehead bulged too. Just above his eyebrows, he thought he could see a ridge forming. Not very noticeable when he looked into the mirror, but he could feel the tightness to where it made his eyelids hard to close completely. When he rubbed, he could feel the rise just above the eyebrows and then slope down again onto his smooth forehead. Apparently it was not very noticeable to others. At least his teammates had not said anything to him about it. He started wearing a ball cap everywhere he went to hide the hump. He was now wearing a size 8. Four sizes more than his regular cap size.

Brad's teammates also stonewalled the press when they wanted to talk about Brad, deferring questions to the manager, Bob Startlin. When cornered, a typical respond was, "hey, whatever he's doing,

I just hope he keeps doing it until after we've won the World Series."

On one occasion, Bob was asked by a local Detroit reporter, "How do you feel about Brad recovering in time for the playoffs?" His reply was, "Brad's always has been a hard worker. His workout regimen is unmatched. He wanted to play in the post season so badly this year, that he dedicated himself to getting back and being in the best possible shape. He knows what it takes to be a champion, so he's gone out and showed us all how much he is willing to work to be that champion."

"It looks to me like it's more than just working out. He looks like those guys back in baseball's Steroid days."

"Brad is drug tested, as are all the players, twice a week during the playoffs. He has passed all of the tests with flying colors, so I think we can rule out steroids or any other flavor of miracle drug. The drug testing is very sophisticated and not one abuser has escaped getting caught in over 10 years. The tests are pretty thorough as they check for over 200 banned substances. I think if he were juiced, the test would catch him, don't you? If he were doing something illegal, we would find it out pretty quickly, don't you think?"

That particular interview came to a sudden end, with Bob ducking into his office and slamming the door hard behind him.

Marisa was scared. She had watched Brad grow these three weeks since returning from Chicago. He had passed his body's growth off as a result of hard workouts and his face as a result of nerves due

168

to the post season, but she suspected something else was happening. His features were becoming abnormal. He kept a shirt on these days, but when he slept she would study the size of his expanded chest and arms. She could make out the various muscle groups in his upper arms and shoulders. Even bodybuilders' muscles relax to normal size when they are not being flexed, but Brad's muscles always appeared taut.

His face was what alarmed her the most. When she stared at him while he slept, his face was constantly twitching. Not twitching in the normal sense, she thought, like an occasional tic, a rapid blink, a curling of his lip, but it actually looked like his face was crawling. Crawling! She shuddered at the thought, but that's what it looked like to her. A twitch is random and unorganized, like a splash, but the movements of his face looked more organized, like his entire face had a twitch. Sometimes, she could see his cheek pulsate in and out, in a rhythmic manner. Not a large movement, but one she is certain she saw.

On a recent off day, an off day because the Tigers had already qualified for the World Series and the National League title was still undecided, Marisa and Brad were lounging in the apartment, and she tentatively asked Brad about his face.

"Just nerves, hon, you know how I get when the playoffs come around."

"It looks to be more than that this time Brad. I can see a noticeable swelling in your cheeks."

"Probably from scratching and rubbing so hard," he shrugged her off. "Doc gave my some antihistamines and I think that's helped

169

quite a bit. My face doesn't itch so much and I'm sure the swelling will go down fast."

"When did you start taking it?" she pressed on.

"Couple days ago."

"Shouldn't the swelling have started to go down by now?"

"I must be extra nervous this year. Probably cuz I was unsure if I was going to be able to contribute or not. But don't worry; the swelling will start to go down, probably tomorrow."

"Have you talked to the Institute about it?"

"Sure, I talk to them every day. They don't seem to be worried and agree the antihistamine will probably take care of it."

"What do they say about your forehead swelling?"

"My forehead, who said anything about that?" he shot back defensively.

"I'm saying it now, Brad your forehead is starting to puff up above your eyebrows. Now don't tell me THAT is nerves?"

Brad didn't like where this conversation was headed, "I got bumped on a slide the last game, it's a little tender," he said giving his brow a rub. "But other than that it's ok, Quit worrying."

"A slide, huh? That's bullcrap Brad, your heads been growing for a week. You're starting to look like a Neanderthal. What's doc said about that?"

"Will you get off my case." He finished the discussion by grabbing his ball cap; forcefully giving it a tug to fit it onto his enlarged head, and left the room.

Later, when Brad was out, she looked up the number of the Institute on the Web.

"Gupta Institute, how may I help you", the sweet female voice on the other end answered.

"I would like to talk to Dr. Gupta please."

"Is Dr. Gupta expecting your call?"

"No, he is not."

"I'm sorry ma'am; Dr. Gupta does not take calls without an appointment. If you would like to speak to someone else or perhaps send an email to the Institute info mailbox, someone will get back to you. Good day."

"Wait, wait. I must talk to the doctor. You see it's not about me, but about my fiancée."

"I'm sorry miss......."

"But something's gone wrong," she quickly interrupted, "something has gone terribly wrong and I must talk to the doctor, I must."

"Sorry ma'am, I'm going to hang up now, have a nice day."

"But he has to help!"

"Goodbye miss."

"He has to help Brad!"

There was a click on the line. Marisa didn't think it sounded like a phone being replaced on its cradle, but a different sound. She was also certain the line was still open as she had not gotten the dial tone.

Her instinct was confirmed when, after a few long seconds, the receptionist was back on the line.

"Miss, you say it's about Brad? Brad who?"

"Brad Dickson, my fiancé, that's what I've been trying to tell you. It's about Brad, I think something is wrong."

A few moments later, a voice with a soft Indian accent came on the line.

"Hello, this is Dr. Gupta, how may I help you?"

"Hello, Doctor, my name is Marisa Martin, I am Brad Dickson's fiancée, I was at the Institute last month when Brad was having a procedure done."

"Yes, Miss Martin, I remember you. How can I help you today?"

"I'm worried about Brad. He is getting large."

"What do you mean "large"?"

"I mean all of him. It started in his thighs, the muscles just kept getting larger. Then his calves started bulging out, like I'd never seen before, then his chest and arms. They're huge. He's huge. He keeps telling me it's because he has been working out so hard but I know he's lying. Then a couple of days ago, I noticed his face has started to swell. It looked at first like he just had hives, you know, due to the post season coming up, his nerves and all, at least that's what he's been saying. But now I've noticed his forehead is starting to grow. Just above his eyebrows. It looks like someone hit him on the forehead with a bat, but there's no bruising, no color,

172

just the swelling. The skin on his face is as tight as a drum, like he's had the world's worst facelift. I know it isn't hives. I think something went wrong with what he had done at your Institute."

"Now, Miss Martin, I assure you there is an explanation for what you are seeing. Perhaps Mr. Dickson is telling you the truth. The growth is due to his vigorous workouts. As you surely know, he had a large amount of muscle damage. We are very surprised frankly; we were able to help him at all. Perhaps he realizes his playing days are numbered so he is trying extra hard to delay that inevitability. Perhaps he really is working out harder than he ever has before. We have repaired his quadriceps muscle quite satisfactorily, perhaps that is making him able to work out longer and harder."

"But what about the Frankenstein look, huh? How do you build up your forehead, with eye lifts? How do you explain that, doctor?"

"Perhaps Mr. Dickson injured himself. Did you ask him about it?"

"Yes, he said he got hit on a slide."

"There, you see, there is the answer."

"But I think he's lying. There is no bruising, no scrape, and no evidence at all of him getting hit. In fact, now that I think about it, He hasn't had to slide into a base since he's returned."

Dr. Gupta was waving his arms frantically and finally caught the attention of his secretary. He motioned her over while Marisa was speaking, giving her a note and flicking his arm at her to hurry.

"And I see things moving."

This got Dr. Gupta's full attention, "you see what?"

"I see things moving in his face, I mean, it looks like there are things moving in his face, just under the skin, he cheeks go this way and that and sometimes it looks like twitching, but other times it looks organized, kind of like a line of ants, marching under the skin. It's creepy."

"When did you first notice this twitching?"

"A couple of days ago. He was sleeping and I was staring at his face, then all of a sudden his cheeks started moving. Not a twitch, a twitch is quick and in one spot, but I saw both his cheeks moving. Something, or at least it looked like something, crawling under the surface. It was frightening. It went on for the longest time, maybe a couple of minutes, then it stopped. I stared at him for a few more minutes, but nothing."

"Did Mr. Dickson wake up during this movement?"

"No, he turned his head a little, but that's it. What is it doc? What's happening?"

I do not know Miss Martin."

Dr. Childress rushed into the room. Dr. Gupta put his index finger to his mouth and Dr. Childress slowed and slowly walked to Dr. Gupta. Dr. Gupta pushed the speaker button on his phone, "Miss Martin, do you think Brad is aware of this twitching?"

"I know he is doctor. Like I said, he told me it was hives, you know, from nerves due to the playoffs, and he started by putting Skin So Soft on his face. Then just yesterday he told me Doc, uh, Dr. Lewis, the team doctor, gave him an antihistamine. But I know it's not helping and I think Brad knows it's not helping. His cheeks just keep getting bigger."

"Is he scratching his forehead?"

"No, I haven't seen him do that yet, but he rubs it. I've caught him rubbing it and then he'll see me looking and quickly stop, like he's hiding the fact that he's rubbing it."

"Miss Martin, do you think I could speak to Mr. Dickson?"

"He's not here right now, he's at the clubhouse, I think. Maybe he's in the weight room, working out. They don't have a game today, so he may be there a while."

"Do you have an idea of when he might return? I really should speak to him and ask about these things you have told me about."

"He sometimes comes home in the late morning to take a quick nap before going back to the stadium for batting practice or whatever."

"Very good, perhaps I will catch him at that time. Miss Martin, did Brad tell you how the procedure went? How the outcome of the procedure went?"

"He said it went great. If fact, he said it went so well, you released him a day early."

Dr. Gupta shot Dr. Childress a concerned glance, took a deep breath and said, "Miss Martin, please listen to me and listen carefully. We think Brad is in trouble. Brad was not released early, he escaped, what I mean to say is, he left the Institute before we had a chance to examine him one last time. We need your help. Would you like to help us help him?"

"Yes, of course. If Brad is in danger I want to do anything I can to help. What do you want me to do?"

175

After leaving the house, instead of going to the stadium, Brad went to Barry's office, which was nearby.

When he walked in, Barry looked at him in horror. "What in the hell happened to you?"

Brad pulled his cap down over his eyes further and rubbed his cheek, "It's nothing, just nerves I guess."

"You guess? Have you looked in the mirror my friend? You look like that guy, uh, who was it, yeah, Peter Boyle in that old Frankenstein movie. Brad, what is going on?"

Brad took his hat off slowly. His frontal lobes jutted out an inch beyond his forehead. His cheeks were bright red and full round, stretched tight, as if they were going to pop. The muscles in his neck were swollen and contorted to where it looked like the t-shirt he had on was about to choke him.

"You are a mess my friend."

"Barry, something wonderful has happened to me. When I was in my last days at the Institute, there was a glitch; the nanobots did not end their 'project', as they call it at the Institute. Instead of dying off and leaving my body when the leg was patched up, they continued to do their job, to fix muscles in my body. First they migrated to my right quad, I guess because it was the same exact muscle they were programmed to fix, and they built it up too, although it was in good shape, they build it up and made it stronger. Bar, I was running full gallop for 2 hours and wasn't even winded. You can't imagine how that feels, to be invincible, to never get tired. It was exhilarating! Well, when the guys, uh, bots got done with that leg, it appears they went looking for more work."

"Weren't the people at the Institute worried?"

"Not at first, I don't think. I think they were just like me, wondering where it was going to go. They kept monitoring the bots; each bot has a radioactive signature, so they track their movement on a screen. It's really a map of my body. They can zoom the view down to just an inch or so. Anyway, we started seeing the bots first go to my right leg then they started going to other parts of my body. The miners, um, the bots that gathered the materials for building, the miners were all over scurrying around my whole body looking for stuff."

"Stuff?"

"Yeah, their job is to find proteins, amino acids, stuff needed for the process of creating cells. For me it is muscle cells. But there's another group, called directors. These guys are kind of like managers, their job is to tell the builders where to build, they organize the builders and direct the miners where to deposit the materials. They keep everything nice and tidy. Well, for some reason the directors started dying off. This left the builders and miners to do what they are programmed to do without direction. So they kept mining and building and mining and building. The people at the Institute were starting to get pretty worried about what was going on. I think they thought I was going to sue them or rat them out to the feds or something, so they told me they wanted to kill off the builders and miners to stop the treatment, but I didn't want them to do that because I liked how they were repairing things, you know, making me stronger, like this," showing Barry his 'guns'.

"So I was thinking I didn't want them to do that, then this chick, Alice, snuck into my room and told me what they were really trying to do was to dose me with radiation and kill me. Kill me with radiation poisoning, making it look like a big accidental overdose, just to cover their asses. You see, the procedure was highly illegal and they all could go to prison. But I didn't want them to cover their asses; I wanted the little guys to keep working, to make me Superman. Well, she snuck in later and gave me some technician clothes, distracted the guard and drove me to the car rental. That's when I drove back to Detroit that day unannounced and made sure I was back in the news so the Institute couldn't come after me. I tried to contact Alice to thank her and see if I could pay her back somehow, but she didn't answer her phone for days. I called a buddy at the Tribune and asked him to look into it, see if he could track her down. He called me back this morning and said her body had washed up on shore near Chicago in Lake Michigan. Poor kid, I think she was killed for helping me escape. I've got to keep them away from me. I thought maybe you or Tony maybe knew someone who could lean on them and tell them to back off and leave me alone. Do you think he could help me?"

Barry pondered this information for a brief moment, "I'll call Tony, I know he can help us with the muscle, sorry, no pun intended, and scare these guys into backing off. He's got motivation. But what about your face and neck, my friend, what happens if these bots don't stop?"

179

Rubbing his cheek, Brad looked at his friend and said, "Then I'll not only be Superman, but the Hulk too!"

Chapter 33

The startled guard looked up at the huge man with a dark complexion. He was dressed in a black suit with white shirt and plain red tie. He had just slammed through the outer door at a high rate of speed, with a purpose. The stranger looked around the ceiling of the entry, his gaze going back and forth from corner to corner as if looking for something.

"May I help you?" The guard was new. He replaced Bill who had ended his shift the day of the escape and had not returned. The new guard was big and was not intimidated by the size of the visitor.

"Maybe. I'm looking for Gupta, Rasheesh Gupta," the stranger said gruffly as he approached the guard shack table.

"I'm afraid Dr. Gupta is not taking visitors today, if you would like to call... "

At that instant, the stranger lunged forward grabbed the back of the guard's head and with one quick motion, slammed his face into the table. The loud crack hinting the nose was broken. Still holding on, he jerked the man's head back up, just as the blood began to gush from the guard's nose. The pained wince on his face confirmed the nose was indeed broken.

"I think I just made an appointment, don't you? Where is he?"

The guard pointed to the door behind the shack with the hand that was not trying to hold his nose together.

"Take me". With that, the visitor, still with a handful of the guard's hair marched the guard to the door. He opened it with his free hand

and threw the guard forward with the other and followed him into the room. The sudden burst surprised Dr. Gupta's assistant and she instinctively jumped to her feet.

"Get me Gupta," he said as he threw the guard aside and withdrew an enormous pistol from inside his jacket, "NOW!"

She worked hard to suppress a scream and quickly knocked on Dr. Gupta's door behind her back as she stared frozen at the gunman. She knocked harder a second time.

"What is it, what is the commot...?" Dr. Gupta rushed through the door and froze at the sight of the gun, stopping in mid sentence.

"You Gupta?" said the gunman, letting go of the guard's hair and now raising the gun barrel up to the doctor's face.

"Yes, Yes I am. What is the meaning of this?"

"I'll tell you the meaning...' as he quickly bridged the distance and pushed the doctor back into his office and shut the door.

The bleeding guard collapsed into a chair as the assistant ran into the outer office looking for someone to help.

Back inside Dr. Gupta's office, the gunman continued, "sit down doc, this won't take long."

The gun was still pointed at Dr. Gupta. "I do not think you need to point that at me," Dr. Gupta said, trying to sound calm but his dry mouth sabotaged the effort.

"I'm doin' the talkin' doc. Now sit down I have a story to tell ya."

The doctor backed to his desk, eyes glued to the gun pointing at him, and slowly lowered himself into his chair. The gunman grabbed the chair in front and sat down. He relaxed his arm and lowered the gun to the top of the desk, where he set it down, rubbed his hands together and began to talk.

"You see doc, it's like this, recently you had a guest here, a Mr. Dickson I believe, a ballplayer, who had a bum leg when he got here and you did some kind of hocus pocus to him and badabing badaboom, his leg is better and he's back in business. He's feeling good enough to play again, and it just so happens, his team, the Tigers, are in the playoffs. Before he went down, the Tigers were 4 to 1 to win the World Series. When Mr. Dickson got hurt, since he's the main man on the team, the odds were moved to 50 to 1, just ahead of the Cubs. Well Mr. Dickson, he approaches my boss and no else knows it yet, but tells him he's ready to play and he's about ready to announce it. So my boss likes to make money too, just like you", he said looking around at the pricey artwork displayed on the walls. "So he asks Mr. Dickson how good he feels and Dickson says he's stronger than any human and his return will assure the Tigers the title. So at 50 to 1, my boss thinks there may be a chance to make a little money. So he goes ahead and puts 2 mil on the Tigers to win.

Then a couple days ago, we get a call from Mr. Dickson's associate who tells us you are trying to keep him from getting better. My boss don't think much of that idea, you see, he don't like people interfering with his business. He thinks Mr. Dickson shouldn't be worried about you interfering with his recovery and he thinks you should give Mr. Dickson all the support you can, as if your life depended on it."

With that, he grabbed the pistol from the desk and held it up and pointed it again at the doctor. Dr. Gupta stiffened and nearly wet himself.

"Did you like that story doc?" He rose from the chair, turned toward the door, grabbed the handle, turned back and said, "I hope for your sake, it has a happy ending," and walked calmly out the door.

He tipped his hat to the assistant who was applying a wet towel to the guard's battered face, "G'day, ma'am," and disappeared out the door.

Chapter 34

Marisa was scared now. Brad's face continued to swell. His body muscles looked proportionate, but they were also large, larger than she could have imagined. While Brad was asleep she went into the study, shut the door and dialed.

"Gupta Institute. How may I help you?"

"Hello, this is Marisa Martin, Brad Dickson's fiancée, is the doctor in? It is very important that I speak to him."

"Just a moment, Ms. Martin, the doctor will be with you shortly."

"This sure is different than the last time I tried to talk to him", she said aloud into the phone.

"Hello Ms. Martin, Dr, Gupta here how may I help you?"

"Dr. Gupta, thank you for taking my call. It's Brad, doctor. I think now he is in very serious trouble."

"How is that Ms. Martin?"

"His face is growing and growing. His cheeks are puffed out. He can hardly close his mouth all the way. And that's just the beginning. His brows are forming a grotesque hump clear across his forehead. He looks hideous. Like Frankenstein's monster. I'm scared doctor, what can you do?"

Remembering the recent visit from Brad's 'friend', Dr. Gupta was hesitant to respond. "Have you discussed your concern with Mr. Dickson?"

"I've tried, but he won't talk about it or he says he feels great and he's going to be the strongest man alive and all this nonsense about living forever and, and…..it is scaring the hell out of me doctor, pardon my French. What's happening to him?"

"Miss Martim, I am not at liberty to help Mr. Dickson, but I will tell you this. You are correct, Mr. Dickson is in trouble. He is in serious trouble. Right now he feels great because the machines in his body are making him better, making him stronger, but soon, very soon, the process will come to an end. All the skeletal muscles will be repaired, enhanced, enlarged to a perfect form. When that happens, if the nanos in Mr. Dickson's body are not neutralized and irradiated, they may possibly attack, and yes I do say attack, his cardiac muscle. The cardiac, the largest muscle in the body is responsible for pumping blood through the heart as I'm sure you are well aware. What you may not know is the cardiac muscle does not benefit from being too large. What happens in a normal person is the cardiac muscle through growing into an adult, strikes a balance of being the proper size for each individual. It is much more complex than the other muscles of the body and we do not yet know what throttles this process as one grows. We suspect there are many factors at play, the size of the body, the width of the blood passages, and the activeness of the individual through the formative years. All of these factors cause the cardiac muscle to not be too big, not too small, but just right to regulate the blood flow through an individual. We do know all too well what happens when that muscle becomes too big for the job. It starts pumping higher volumes of blood causing hypertension, or high blood pressure. This can cause a number of side effects, including coronary heart disease, kidney failure, stroke, and heart failure.

186

That is only the beginning. It also will cause cardiomegaly, or to laymen, a weak heart. The muscle will become stiff and thick and function inefficiently. When the heart enlarges, it works harder and untreated, can quickly lead to heart failure.

Brad has a double problem, due to the increased size of his skeletal muscles. His body needs to pump more blood through to replenish the increased usage of oxygen by his muscles. At the same time, if his heart is growing, it is becoming weaker and less able to supply the blood. This opposing situation could quickly lead to heart failure if untreated."

"Do you think Brad's heart muscle is being attacked?"

"It is very possible, I am afraid. There is nothing to stop the nanos from continuing to repair. If they recognize the heart as being just another muscle, they will go about making it the biggest and strongest heart muscle they can. If this does occur, Mr. Dickson is in serious trouble without treatment."

"How would you know if it is occurring?"

"Symptoms would begin with a tingling sensation in the chest punctuated by sharp pains. Does he complain of discomfort in his chest area?"

"He has lately been rubbing it, writing it off as nerves due to the playoffs."

"Has he had sharp pains, needle pokes in his chest?"

"I've seen him flinch a couple of times, like he'd been shocked or something."

"Does the coloring in his face flush to a bright red?"

"His face is very red, swollen and red."

"It sounds like he is experiencing early symptoms of an enlarged heart. Untreated, it will kill him."

"What can I do doctor? He won't listen to reason. He won't seek help."

"I wish I knew young lady, I wish I knew. You need to convince him to get help, to get treatment before these things kill him. We could kill the bots and start him on a treatment regimen immediately, but it has to be Mr. Dickson's choice."

"Thank you, doctor."

"Good luck to you. Call me if he agrees to see us."

Marisa hung up the phone. She looked toward the bedroom. Brad was dozing but she could hear his labored breathing from across the room. She entered the bedroom, approached the bed, and shook him gently.

His eyes opened and after his vision focused, he stared at her, "What? Why did you wake me up?"

"We have to talk, Brad?"

"We do? About what?"

"About you. About this crazy experiment gone bad. You have to do something NOW!"

"What are you talking about? I am fine."

"No, you're not Brad, you are not fine. You are dying."

"HA, where did you get a crazy idea like that?"

"I'm not crazy, I called Dr. Gupta and…."

"You called him? You called him behind my back?"

"I had to do it Brad, I'm getting scared."

"Scared about what? I'm in the best shape of my life I'm in better shape than I ever, ever dreamed. I am far from dying darling, I am being rebuilt. I'll be good for another 100,000 miles."

"No you won't. Dr. Gupta says you are dying and it might be soon," she began to sob uncontrollably. "And you won't even stop it and you are going to die."

"Now settle down sweetie, what makes you think I'm going to die?"

"Dr. Gupta says your heart may be attacked, yes, he used that word, attacked, by the bots and they will make your heart too big and it will quit and you will die. I don't want you to die. Dr. Gupta says if you will come back to the Institute, he will make you better and you won't die. Please Brad, let's go to the Institute."

"Honey, listen, Dr. Gupta is lying to you. He is covering his ass. You see, he performed a procedure on me he should not have done. They had never injected nanos into humans, just petri dishes and lab animals. He got greedy. I offered him a lot of money to help me and he couldn't refuse. Their science is good. I'm proof, but he got cold feet when I told him I was going to leave the clinic and tell my wonderful story of being healed by their work. But this would have been bad for him, as non-FDA approved trials could mean shutting down the Institute and long jail sentences for the good doctor and all his assistants. So despite the prospect of recognition, he had to shut down the experiment. Luckily, I learn

189

about his plan to stop it and escaped, yes I said escape. They had the place locked down when I left. I think they had planned to kill me.

So you see, Dr, Gupta has every reason to convince you that my health is in jeopardy. He is trying to use you to get me to return, so he can remove any evidence. Maybe even remove me too. But I know better. I've been a professional athlete for 20 years and nobody knows their body or its functioning better than I. And I tell you I feel great. So please no more discussions with Dr. Gupta and no more talk of dying. I'm going to live forever."

He hopped out of bed and left Marisa there, crying.

Chapter 35

It had turned into a good series. The Tigers and Cards each having won 3 games, and finally, as some had predicted, it was going to come down to this seventh and final game. The Tigers had played a solid series with their suddenly invincible captain leading the way. A .543 average, with 7 homers and 17 runs batted in were all time World Series records, and Brad and the boys still had one more game to play. The only thing that stretched this series beyond 4 games was the ineffective pitching staff of the Tigers. The starters were having a rough series and the bullpen, an even rougher one. Despite lousy pitching, Brad's single-handed output had delivered Detroit to the threshold of another World Championship.

Brad kept away from the press and the peering eyeballs of the television networks. He did not want to answer questions about the changes in his appearance. There were rumors and speculation that spanned the gamut; from a rare disease to stem cell injections to voodoo and witch doctors. Before the Series' games, he had stayed behind in the clubhouse until the last minute to take the field. Every time he emerged from the dugout, he could feel all the cameras in press row, with their zoom lenses snapping shots of him and sending the images to their copy desks. As he looked around the stadium, he could always pick out at least 4 of the television cameras pointed at him. He was sure the announcers discussed his physical appearance at every chance. He didn't care. The bots continued to develop the muscles in his body. All physical functions were now done with the greatest of ease and nothing could make him breathe hard or affect his stamina. He was a marvel, and he knew it. The bat at the plate felt like a chopstick and swinging it required almost no exertion. His eyes were still 37 years old, so he didn't always put good wood on the ball, but when he did, there was no doubt where the ball was going to end up. Usually 500 feet in the opposite direction from which it had been pitched. Much to the delight of Tiger fans and the chagrin of the Cards faithful.

There were calls from every direction for Brad to be drug tested and even to suspend him until the truth came out. The Cards manager, Bud Albert, went so far as to file a protest after game 4 when Brad connected for 4 gigantic home runs. The commissioner's office had rejected that appeal, but there was still pressure for Brad to reveal what had happened. He continued to insist there was no drugs involved and that it was just his grueling rehab effort and renewed enthusiasm for the game. Concerning his ever-growing facial distortions, he allowed that it was unusual, maybe some kind of reaction to the stress of the Series, and that he'd undergo thorough testing once the season was over.

Out of view of the cameras and the public, he was worried about his facial appearance. The muscles in his face were so taut, he had trouble chewing food and closing his eyes. But he sensed the swelling had slowed down and that gave him comfort that the repair to those muscles must be finished, or at least just about over. His calves, thighs, arms, torso, shoulders were all well developed and huge. He sensed that the growth had finally stopped. Perfect size, he thought, INVINCIBLE.

Marisa could not bear to look at his face. She had tried to convince him two more times to talk to Dr. Gupta but had failed. She had a rendezvous worked out with Dr. Gupta, during an off day in the series, but at the last moment, he had called her and said he was not coming and he was not going to try to help Brad any more. He said if Brad was so determined to continue to grow bigger, he no longer would be able to save him. Dr. Gupta, during their last conversation had warned Marisa that the bots were probably still alive and actively looking for work, He cautioned her that it was now 5 weeks since the injection and though the bots should have expired two weeks earlier, it appeared by the continued growth of Brad's body and especially his face, that they probably would not die without some type of intervention. He warned the only muscle it appeared they had not inspected was his heart muscle. Dr. Gupta said he hoped the bots would not recognize it as a muscle, but again explained to her what the outcome of an enlarged heart muscle would be. She tried in vain to get Brad to understand the danger. He told her the bots had stopped building his muscles and were probably dead or dying. She hoped he was right.

Before each of the playoff games, Brad was able to hide out in the clubhouse, and would stay there until just before the game started. Then he would dart onto the field, with his ball cap pulled down over his eyes as low as he could pull it and still be able to see. He had to have a special cap made so he could pull it down over his brow's protuberance. During the last game when his hat blew off in a sudden wind gust, he heard the gasps in the crowd and the cameras clicking before he could get the cap back on his head. In the New Star Review paper the next day, was a full front page picture of him with the caption, "Is Brad Dickson The Missing

193

Link?" And that wasn't even the worst one. The press and especially the tabloids were having a good time at his expense.

No one could make fun of his production however. His bat silenced his detractors at least during the games.

On this day, he had gotten up feeling a strange tingling in his chest. Marisa caught him rubbing it, "What's wrong?"

"Nothing," he said quickly pulling his hand away and pulling the shirt down.

"Not nothing, you were rubbing your chest, does it hurt?"

"No, it's nothing really, just had an itch that's all. Don't be so paranoid."

"It didn't look like you were scratching an itch; it looked like you were rubbing your chest. You had a worried look on your face."

"No, you are wrong. I was just thinking about the game tonight. How we've worked so hard all season to be in this position. I was thinking about how Meyers will probably try to pitch to me, stuff like that. I just rubbed my chest out of habit, I guess."

"You would tell me if something was wrong, wouldn't you baby?"

"Sure I would. It's nothing, I swear."

Brad recalled the conversation as he sat in the locker room in front of his locker. His mind and heart were racing, just one more game, just a few more hours and we'll repeat as champions of the world. Then I can relax and let my body rest. Yes, that's it, what's best way to have muscles atrophy? Do nothing, I'll just do nothing, I

194

will not move my face at all, then the muscles will shrink and my face will return to normal. That's it. Got to make sure the bots are gone though, or they'll just keep building it up. But how? Maybe after the series I'll have Tony call off the dogs and make nice with Dr. Gupta and have the Institute remove the bots. Just one more game, one more day that's all I need.

He looked at the clock, 20 minutes until game time. He could hear the volume of the crowd growing as the stadium filled. He vaguely comprehended the public announcer's plea for the fans to eat and drink heartily at the many venues in the stadium. He could hear his teammates in the adjacent room talking to each other words of encouragement. He wished he could join them, but Bob thought it was better this way. His appearance was distracting the others from concentrating on their game.

He had always been the cheerleader, the motivator, in the locker room. Now he was just the freak show making a cameo appearance, knock the snot out the ball, return to the dugout, and disappear down the ramp, out of view of the ever-present network cameras. He began pacing. He stopped in front of a mirror and inspected his face. I think it's actually gone down today; he tried to convince himself, as he unconsciously rubbed his bloated brow.

Ten minutes until game time. The rest of his teammates were funneling out of the locker room and making way through the tunnel to the home dugout. He would join them shortly. Just three more hours and it will be over. He could rest, relax, and he hoped, enjoy the feeling of being a world champion again. He realized he had rarely thought of Mr. Yorkey in the past week. Ever since the series started, the owner had kept away from the dugout and the team. He normally was right in the middle of things, but this time he was nowhere to be seen. OK by Brad. He'd have his fun with Yorkey during the winter. He wondered how the conversation would go when he told Yorkey he was going to file for free agency. He could not wait to see the look on his face. He felt bad in a way, Yorkey had brought him into the bigs, but that was ancient history. What Yorkey had done last month was unforgivable, and he'd make him regret it too.

Brad heard the announcer ask the crowd to rise for the National Anthem. Almost time. He'd wait until it was over before heading for the dugout. It's always better to be the home team, he thought. You don't have to sit on the bench when the game starts. You get out there in the field and immediately get involved. No time to sit and think about what's going on, you just go out and do it, out of habit, out of instinct. These last few days it had been even better, since he went to the dugout just before the games started. Even less time to sit and think about it.

He hadn't needed much warming up time ever since his return. His arm was always loose, his aim was true, and his throw was strong.

The Anthem ended to a thunderous roar. It was time. He grabbed his glove and made his way to the dugout.

He pulled his hat down tight one last time, took a deep breath and hopped the three steps and on to the field to join the rest of his team. The crowd noise muffled for a brief instant when he appeared, but then returned to the painful decibel level it had been. He positioned himself at third, swept the dirt in front of him with his left foot, and then back the other way with his right. He pulled once more on the bill of his cap to make sure it was as low as possible.

At last, he was on the field. It was always that first instant of leaving the safety of the dugout when the nerves hit. His nerves immediately started to settle. Brad was deep in thought. In there, in the dugout, most of the fans could not see you or see what you were doing. But once you stepped foot onto the field, all eyes were on you watching every move you made. You couldn't scratch or rub any body part, which always seemed to need scratching or rubbing, for fear it would end up on the front page in the morning, or go viral on YouTube.

He was in position. Taking grounders from the first baseman and effortlessly firing strikes back at him. He could hear the conversations of the fans near the third base line, but with so many chattering; he could not make out what was being said. Were they talking about him? Probably. He looked up in the crowd, thousands talking, sitting, standing, arms waving, eating, every one of them ready for the game. Ready to celebrate the athletes' achievements, equally ready to boo the flaws, the humanness of the players. Cameras were ready, pointing, many aimed at him, snapping his picture with a machine-gun like cadence. In the booth, the commentators were surely talking about Brad. Talking about his accomplishments. Talking about his achievements. Talking about the tear he was on. Talking about tonight's game. Talking about his appearance. Talking about the bulk of his body, about the hugeness of his muscles. Hoping to get a glimpse of history.

Deep in his own thoughts, Brad thought, maybe, just maybe, he will achieve something tonight never achieved before. Perhaps a five home run game. Not very likely though, as Myers is one of the best pitchers around.

There is no way I'll get up five times tonight, he thought. But three homers, yeah, three is definitely doable. If they don't walk me. Or maybe I'll falter. Some would like that. Some people will want to see me fail. Certainly the Cards fans, but there are others too, many, maybe millions, just waiting for me to screw up. Somehow it seems to make people happy, like they themselves have accomplished something when someone else fails. Human nature. Always rooting against someone or something. See how ready they are to point out my flaws, my fallacies? Talking about the deformity my face has become. Wondering, as many do, what has caused this to happen? What will happen next? Will my skin turn green? Will I suddenly rip through my shirt? Why has a normal person suddenly become a hideous monster? Does it add to the mystique of the game? Does it transcend me to the realm of an ogre? Do any of them know? Do any of them really know what it means to sacrifice? Do any of them know how much effort it took me to get to this point? Are they aware I am right now, probably the best EVER at what I do? They think they know. They think they can relate. They take my achievements and try to superimpose them on their own lives and tell themselves "yeah', I could do that if given the chance'. But they had been given the chance, the same chance I was given. They were born a healthy person, with two arms, two legs. They had the same chance growing up to become good at the game. They chose, for whatever reason, to not pursue perfection on the baseball field. They were distracted; they found other things to do. They didn't spend every single waking hour honing their skill. But here they were, ready to judge me, ready to criticize me for my effort, for my sacrifice, for my commitment. They know not the first idea of what it takes to get to this level. To stay here. To be the best of the best. How dare they point at my deformed face and judge!

One more grounder. Fire it back to the first baseman. Yeah that felt good, the arm is loose the aim is true. Let's get this going. Let's put on a show for the non-achievers so they can talk about it tomorrow at work. They have not sacrificed. They have not fought through adversity, but they will be glad to help take the glory that will be given to the victor. They will be equally ready to cast the blame of defeat on our failure to prepare, our failure to concentrate, our failure to care about the outcome as much as they care. But when it's over, after a week or two, they will be on to a different sport, to idolize or criticize another team, another athlete, while the true athlete is left to ponder every minute of every game for the rest of their life. To relive the triumph, but more often, the defeat, over and over again. No matter what is done in the future, the past cannot be forgotten, nor can it be changed. The participant cannot remove himself from the outcome, any more than they can change it. If an opportunity is lost or squandered, the event is replayed over and over, each day. Then again at night as the person is lying in bed wide awake, unable to sleep, unable to shake the feeling of that which was not achieved. Reliving the event, over and over. Imagining how a fraction of an inch or a second could have changed their history, their legacy, their ability to look at themselves in the mirror with pride and know they achieved the feat, or with dread and knowing they will always be associated with the failure.

Please, on this night, please allow me to achieve the victory. To quiet my critics, my distracters. To let me enjoy this moment of rising to the pinnacle with a superb and perfect effort. To make all the years of sacrifice and preparation come to fulfillment on this field of battle. To quiet the little people who know nothing of sacrifice, but are quick to point out the sacrifice was not good enough. Let me quiet these unknowing bandwagoners. Let me be! He visibly shook his head to clear his thoughts.

Aaron Hanrady, the Detroit Tigers starter, number 27, delivered the first pitch, a ball, and at last, thought Brad, the game has started. I can focus my energy on it, and not on the multitudes of people thinking about everything BUT the game.

The first inning went quickly, when the Detroit pitcher settled in and threw strikes. Brad had an easy first inning in the field and was not involved in any play.

When the Tigers came to bat in the bottom of the first, the fans were on their feet, roaring their support for the home team. Brad was due up third and immediately put on his batting helmet, which had been recently enlarged. He hurried into the dugout, looking away from the nearest camera so it could not capture too much of his face to study. Sayers, the first batter, had a quick 4 pitch strikeout and next to the plate was Jackson. When Brad climbed out of the dugout to take his position in the on-deck circle, with two bats in hand, a roar when up throughout the stadium. He was aware of the cheer but dared not acknowledge it. He closely watched the opposing pitcher, Brandon Myers, trying to get a sense of his delivery, of his rhythm. Brad had only faced him in the opening game of the Series and did not see many strikes, but knew all about him from the years he had pitched in the National League. Add to that, the numerous notes in the scouting report that Bob had gone over with the team that afternoon, and not least of all, the first time they saw him in the series, a game the Tigers lost.

"Strike one," called the umpire.

The second pitch was delivered. A fast ball, he guessed from his perspective in the on-deck circle. He had timed his swing to coincide with the pitch. Brad felt he was right on the pitch and felt confident he would do well against Myers. Brad thought the pitch was too high and guessed a ball would be called.

"Strike two."

Jackson backed out and with raised eyebrows, took a hard look at Dykstra, the umpire, who stood motionless, expressionless, with hands on his hips.

Brad got ready, bat on his shoulder, just as if he were in the box.

The third pitch was delivered. This time, a slider, somewhat inside but Jackson took a hard cut at it and got nothing but air for the effort.

As Jackson walked past Brad, he said, "Watch it Brad, Dykstra's strike zone is high tonight."

Brad stepped up to the plate. The fans rose from their seats in a unified chaotic frenzy of cheers and whistles.

Brad dropped his right foot into the box, gave it a couple of twists and brought the left foot up, just inside the front chalk. He took a couple of practice swings, the whole time staring at Myers who was returning the gaze. Myers nodded his approval of the catcher's sign and began the windup. Brad cradled the bat on his right shoulder and tightened his grip on the bat. The pitch was launched.

Brad had always had a knack for instantly determining the pitch by the rotation as it left the pitcher's hand. That's what separated him from an average major league hitter. This one was definitely a slider and he mentally adjusted his timing to coincide what he thought the speed of the pitch was going to be. It looked to be in the strike zone, in an area he had trained himself to look for hittable pitches. He uncocked the bat and drove it through the strike zone with a furiously quick swat. He barely missed the mark and harmlessly fouled the pitch straight back into the backstop. Good, he thought to himself as he stepped out of the box following the backswing, I'm right on the speed; I just misjudged the drop on his slider. Got to keep my swing level through the zone next time.

Had it been a good slider, there's a pretty good chance Brad would be trotting around the bases by now.

The umpire threw a new ball out to the Cards ace. He took his glove hand out of the mitt and rubbed the ball hard with both hands. Brad was mentally analyzing what the next pitch would be. He knows I've got the speed down, just a little low on the location. Will he come back with the same pitch, a little higher to see if I'll climb the ladder with him? Or will he go to a different speed? Maybe a fastball? Will it be inside or outside? Brad peeked at the catcher's position, who did not have a target up yet, unwilling to give away the battery's strategy. Brad stepped back in. Myers was ready. He shook off one sign, and then nodded to the next. The crowd grew quiet in anticipation and the pitch was delivered. It

202

was a fastball, outer half, belt high. Brad, looking for another off-speed pitch didn't like the rotation he saw on the ball coming out of the pitcher's' hand and decided not to swing. The ball caught the outside corner and Fred Dykstra emphatically yelled 'strike two'. Forty-thousand moans were followed immediately by a crescendo of boos.

Brad stepped out of the box and glared back at Dykstra, who returned Brad's stare with one of his own and motioned Brad to get back into the batter's box.

Brad refocused and wondered what the next pitch would be. Myers drew a lot of strikeouts by coming back inside with a late breaking slider, he recalled the briefing notes he studied earlier, moving the right-handed batter off the plate as the ball curled back over the strike zone.

Brad knew what was coming and was prepared for it. The pitch was delivered, spin was right and Brad knew it was going to break low. I'm all over it, he thought, as he cocked his bat, dropped his right shoulder and began the swing. As he had predicted, the ball started low and began to break late, starting out like it would hit his knee and then started breaking across the plate. Brad dipped his body as he started the swing. Unfortunately, this slider did not bite and stayed up. Brad's bat hit the ball with full force, but a little lower on the ball than square and he hit a towering fly to second base. The second baseman stood motionless for the longest moment, eyes fixed straight up in the air. Finally the harmless fly ball landed in his glove, and he closed it tight with his non-glove hand. The second base umpire made the unneeded 'out' sign by raising his right hand as the ball dropped into the glove. The crowd let out a collective groan and the side was retired. Brad had rounded first by the time the ball was caught. He turned and glanced at the front row fans beyond the first base dugout as he trotted to first and saw their collective look of disappointment. A smattering of St. Louis Cardinal fans, in their bright red jackets and sweatshirts, rose and cheered.

The game became a pitcher's duel. The Cards pushed a run across in the fourth on a walk, sacrifice bunt and a timely single. That was the only run of the game through six and a half innings. Brad had hit the ball hard on his next at bat but right at the left fielder.

The home crowd was getting nervous and became noticeable quiet as the game progressed. The game was moving fast and the home team didn't have much to show for it. The Tigers had a double to lead off the fifth inning, but a couple of timely strike outs and a rally ending diving catch by the left fielder left the game a 1-0 Cardinal advantage.

As the second baseman threw over to first to record the last out in the top of the seventh, Brad began to think of his upcoming at bat. He was due up first in the seventh. He had gotten some good cuts against Myers but had bad luck each time. As he ran off the field he felt a slight flush and tingling in his chest. He pulled his shoulders back and stretched his chest. The tingling stopped as he walked down the stairs. He threw his glove on the bench, grabbed his batting helmet and bat, and returned up the stairs to the on-deck circle. He picked up the donut and began to swing the bat from side to side. A fan in the front row, right behind the on-deck circle yelled "C'mon Dickson hit the damn ball this time. We need a run."

Through years of being a pro, Brad ignored the fan, not giving him the satisfaction of acknowledgement. But he heard him, like he always hears them. "WE need a run?" What position do you play on the team? WE? What gives you the right to demand a run for OUR team? Just because you are rich enough to get that front row seat, that does not give you the right to demand anything of me, and certainly not the right to say 'WE'. Brad bent down and grabbed some dirt and rubbed it along the handle. What he really wanted to do was smack the guy upside the head with his bat.

The crowd rose as one and stood quietly at attention as an officer in the United States Army came out to home plate and sang "God Bless America". There was a sense of excitement at the conclusion because everyone knew Brad was going to lead off the bottom of the seventh, and he was due for a hit.

Down one to nothing, he could afford to take home run cuts at the ball. A single here most likely wouldn't help much, not with the handcuff Myers was putting on his team tonight. When the catcher threw to second, Brad strode confidently up to the plate.

He figured, well maybe hoped, that Myers was wearing down some. His fastball had lost a couple miles per hour since the beginning of the game and he had been taking more time between pitches the last couple of innings. Brad went to the plate looking for a slider about belt high over the inside of the plate that he could drive. He reckoned Myers would try to get the first pitch in for a strike to create a pitcher's count.

The first pitch was delivered, and as he had guessed it was a slider about belt high. Brad cocked and swung through the plate with a furious swing. The bat connected square on the ball and it left the infield headed toward left field at a very high rate of speed.

The crowd grew eerily silent and as one, rose to its feet to watch the liner clear the left field fence, seemingly still on the rise, and ricochet around the home team's bullpen, nearly beaning one of the coaches. The crowd went into an unabashed frenzy as Brad rounded first base, his fist pumping in the air like he was pulling the chord on a subway train. During the entire trip around the bases, the crowd roared its approval. Brad delivered what they had all been anticipating. As he rounded second, he thought of the fan behind the on-deck circle and glance quickly over to him just as he was high fiving his neighbor. Yeah, WE did it buddy, as he stepped down on second base.

Turning past third and low fiving the third base coach, Brad caught sight of all his teammates, gathered around home plate, waiting once again, to welcome him home. As he crossed the plate, the umpire threw a new ball to the pitcher, who circled the mound still talking to himself.

The inning ended three batters later, but Brad had done what he had always done. Gotten that clutch hit at the right time.

As he ran onto the field, the crowd erupted once again in a unified recognition of his feat. He nodded as he crossed the foul line. Maybe now they will quit thinking of how I look and only think of how I play.

Another tingling sensation went through his chest, like a shock, starting high up near his collarbone and continuing down to the area just below his rib cage. This was following by a sharp pain that lasted only an instant, like a quick jab. He rubbed the epicenter of the jab, a spot near the top of his rib cage on his left side. The pinch went away as quickly as it had arrived, but the tingling lingered on and only started to subside when he took up his position at third base.

Coach Startlin had seen enough of Hanrady. Although he was still throwing the ball well and getting outs, his pitch count had reached 123 at the end of the seventh, and Startlin, not wanting to take any chances in this situation with a tie game, brought in his bullpen ace, Julio Velasquez, who had not allowed a run in 39 of the 43 appearances he had made. Velasquez had a mean fastball clocked during the season at one time at 108 miles per hour. Add to this, he had pinpoint control and as if that wasn't enough, to complete the unfair advantage he enjoyed over most hitters, a wicked change up where his delivery looked just like the heater, but came in 30 miles per hour slower, causing many a batter, sitting on the fastball to corkscrew themselves into the ground. He would face the number 9 hitter then the top of the order. His job was to get three quick outs and not allow the Cardinals sluggers to come to the plate.

The inning started easy enough. He got the Card's catcher, Sparky Freeman, on three mean pitches, the last one clocked at 106. Then back to the top of the order. Periwinkle, the Cards second baseman had some luck against Julio earlier in the summer during an interleague game, smacking a double to deep center. He probably felt he had a good chance tonight to do the same, or better. The first pitch to him was low and outside, ball one. The crowd volume inched down a bit as Periwinkle stepped out, adjusted his batting glove straps, and stepped back in.

The second pitch, near the same spot, but more to the liking of the umpire.

"Stee-rike" he bellowed, lurching out to his side and extending his right arm as if lunging in a fencing match.

Periwinkle stepped out, looked down at his third base coach who was clapping his hands, and rubbing various parts of his body, none of which were signs for his batter. Periwinkle readjusted the gloves once more and stepped in.

The next pitch was a patented Velasquez change up. Periwinkle was way out ahead of it and nearly twisted a full turn at the plate. The crowd roared its approval as the slightly embarrassed second baseman stepped out to regroup and gather his thoughts.

On the next pitch, he got a piece of the ball and fouled in off to the first base side of the bleachers, just a few rows up from the dugout.

Two more 105 mile per hour heaters were also fouled off. The count remained 1-2. On the next pitch, Velasquez completely fooled Periwinkle and the audience of millions by throwing a high arching Uncle Charlie that caused Periwinkle to freeze in the box as the baseball arched down into the strike zone.

"Tha-ree, yer out" Dykstra put his hands together and pulled them apart like he was readying his bow to launch an arrow. The crowd erupted in approval as the catcher whipped the ball down to Brad to start the throw around the horn.

Two down. The Card's #2 hitter went down with a lot less drama by feebly whiffing at three hard fastballs in a row.

The Tigers didn't fare any better and their three batters went down without getting the ball out of the infield.

Chapter 36

Top of the ninth. Perhaps it would be the last inning of the year.

The crowd sensed the urgency of the players and stood and cheered their home town boys.

Velasquez had looked good in the eighth and the Tiger faithful had high hopes he could control the Cards in the ninth. It would be a tough assignment as the Cards heart of the lineup was due up.

First to bat was the center fielder, Jared Goth. Goth and Velasquez had never faced each other, and Velasquez won this first encounter by inducing a groundout on a 2-2 pitch. Next up was Alex Bronski. If the Cards needed a hit from their superstar, it was now.

Velasquez pitched Bronski very carefully, not wanting to get beat on a bad pitch and finally walked him after an 11-pitch at bat. Glenn Edwards was next, and although he had rarely bunted during the season, laid down a perfect bunt toward Brad, who fielded it cleanly but had no chance to get Bronski at second, so instead fired a rocket to first to get the sure second out. Two down. The crowd stood as one now as Dirk Lathram came to the plate. He tightened first the batting glove on his left hand, then the right, wiggled his left foot in at the top of the batter's box a couple of times, reached out with his left arm and tapped the bat on the far side of the plate twice, brought his right foot in, just inside the back line, twisted it in for traction, took a couple of swings, and cocked the bat back on his right shoulder and stared out at Velasquez.

For his part of the ritual dance, Velasquez took a deep breath and let it out with an audible hiss, adjusted his cap down further on his forehead so the batter could barely see his eyes, placed his right foot just in front of the pitching rubber, leaned in toward the plate, glove hand on his leg, rotating the ball slowly in his throwing hand, and waited for the catcher's signal. He shook his head slightly and the catcher changed the sign. After a barely perceptible nod, he raised his body up, bringing his left foot next to his right and at the same time, brought his pitching hand into his glove and stopped. He looked over his shoulder as Bronski edged further off of second base. Velasquez froze in that position for an eternity trying to will the runner back toward the bag. The crowd grew silent. Velasquez turned his head back to the batter, who was rocking the bat on his shoulder. The infielders bent over gloves out and ready, on their toes. The Tiger's catcher Harley Jervis crouched down, moving his glove to the lower inside part of the plate, giving his pitching the target for the pitch. Velasquez lifted his left leg high, separated his pitching hand from the glove, dropped it back behind him and motioned forward at the same time he brought his left leg down hard, rotated his body forward and swiftly brought his pitching arm around and let go the pitch. It was headed right at the catcher's glove when Lathram lifted his left leg, rotated his upper body and brought the bat around at high velocity. The ball and bat arrived at a spot above the plate and the cracking sound of the impact could be easily heard in the now silent ball park. The resulting line drive easily cleared the outstretched glove of the leaping second baseman, as it left the infield. The right fielder, moving instinctively at the crack of the bat, was running at full speed but could not get to the ball before it bounced on the outfield grass. He fielded it on the first bounce, cleanly removed the ball from his glove, planted his right foot and heaved it toward

211

the plate. At the crack of the bat, Bronski had taken off and was watching his third base coach, who was wind-milling his left arm, Bronski rounded third at full speed and was on his way home when the right fielder released the ball.

Jervis set up just to the third base side of the plate, blocking it as he readied himself to catch the ball and the inevitable collision with Bronski. Unfortunately for the Tigers, Bronski arrived a split second sooner than the ball and rolled over the catcher as the ball hit him in the back and rolled harmlessly to a stop a few feet away. During the roll, Bronski reached out and touched the plate with his left hand. Dykstra, standing directly over the sprawling players had already given the safe sign as the players came to a halt and the small cloud of dust dissipated.

The Cards dugout erupted in cheers as Bronski hopped to his feet. Velasquez picked up the ball, looked up and saw the runner round second base too far and threw a strike to the second baseman, who put the tag on him for the third out. But the damage had been done. The Cards took the lead 2-1.

Chapter 37

The stadium had grown eerily silent as the teams exchanged positions for the bottom of the ninth inning. Fortunately for the Tigers, the top of their order was due up in the ninth.

Sayers was quickly dispatched when an 0-2 grounder created the first out. Jackson eventually coaxed a 12 pitch walk from Myers and the crowd came to life again. The Cards had seen enough of Myers and with Brad coming to the plate. Their manager, Frank Cuttle, hopped out of the dugout, motioned to the umpire for 'time', and tapped his left arm with his right index finger to signal to the bullpen he wanted his ace left-hand reliever, Pancho Garcia, to face the Tigers star. Garcia had faced Brad a few times and had held him to 1 single in 12 at bats.

Cuttle liked his odds, but also considered walking Brad and taking his chances with the Tiger's clean-up hitter, Chas Baker.

When Perez had reached the mound, Cuttle asked him, "Do you want to pitch to Dickson or put him on and face Baker?"

Confidently, Garcia replied, "I've never had trouble with Dickson, I can get him."

"OK, just do it. Keep it low and outside," Cuttle replied, tossing the ball to him.

Brad stood at the plate, all the work, all the pain, all the unknowns, the fear of trying the procedure, the joy of its success. Now it all boiled down to this. The fate of so many, the future recognition,

213

the wealth generated by the events of the next 30 minutes was unimaginable.

A World Series victory guaranteed each player on the winning team a $200,000 paycheck. But it was more than that. It was the negotiating position of the stars, it was the royalties from merchandise sales, and it was the appearances on the talk shows, to rub elbows with the rich, the famous, and the beautiful people. To be on the winning team of a World Series guaranteed a player a changed life of security and fame. Brad knew all too well what a victory would mean to him and his team. And the hero of such a victory would have riches almost beyond comprehension. Access to the elite of the elite. The most famous actors and actresses in Hollywood would want to hang out with him, have him over for dinner. They'd look up to HIM, instead of being the objects of admiration, they would be the admirers. The hero would receiver all the spoils. Right now that hero was Bronski. Brad had some experience at being a World Series hero and fully intended to take it away from Bronski.

Brad bent down, picked up a handful of dirt, and slowly rubbed it on the handle of his bat. He ignored the tingling in his chest. His adrenaline was flowing too fast, too intense, to allow the tingling to bother him. He knew with one swing of the bat, all he'd done, all he'd endured would be worth it. He took a deep breath, exhaled audibly, and stepped in.

The Card's closer stepped to the side of the rubber, looked in, nodded and fired the ball.

In the most nerve-wracking, tense situations, Brad excelled. He always maintained his even demeanor. He saw the ball leave the pitcher's hand in a slowed reality. He saw the individual stitches as the ball began to spin rapidly as it approached the plate. Brad knew from the direction and speed of the spin the pitch was a split-fingered fastball. In the split second needed, he judged the ball would cross the plate just above his knees. He instinctively bent his knees a little, pivoted back on his right side, turned his hips and at the same time, brought the bat forward to intercept the pitch. Only this time, he misjudged the height of the ball and his club passed harmlessly over the top of it. .

"Stee-rike one", Dykstra empathically shouted, arm extended as always. The catcher returned the ball to the pitcher and pumped his fist in approval.

Brad backed out of the box. He felt his chest tighten. He tightened the straps on his gloves, adjusted the batting helmet and stepped in. The pitcher stepped on the rubber again. Suddenly, Brad felt a sharp pain shoot through his chest like what he thought a Taser must feel like. He raised his right hand for the umpire and was granted time out. He stepped out of the batter's box, and rotated his bat a couple of times. This seemed to ease the intensity of the sharp pain, enough anyway to step back in.

The pitcher got back on the rubber, approved the sign and went into his stretch, glanced back at the runner on first, paused and fired toward home. Brad again saw what he suspected was a split finger and readied his body as the ball made its way to home plate. He pulled the trigger and gave the bat a mighty swing. Contact. The ball left the infield quickly, heading for the left field fence. The crowd, already out of their seats, stopped shouting. For an instant there was a surreal quiet at Comerica. Brad momentarily just watched the ball before remembering to start running. The runner on first took off toward second keeping his eyes on the ball. It looked to him like the left fielder was not going to be able to catch it and he lowered his head and started running in a full gallop. The left fielder had gotten a late start on the ball and was desperately trying to catch up to it as it approached the left field corner. The line umpire turned as the ball went over his head and lined up his sights on the foul line, waiting for the ball to drop. It was his call, foul or fair. The pitcher, upon the crack of the bat, had an agonized look on his face as the projectile quickly left the infield. Brad's teammates as one turned their heads and unconsciously, instinctively, started to climb up the dugout stairs. Bob Startlin, hanging on the rail at the far end of the dugout looked out into the lighted Detroit night sky and picked up the ball's trajectory as it crossed the dirt of the infield into the outfield. Mr. Yorkey, in his box alone, high above the field, watched the ball below him shoot out to left field.

The ball landed in the corner, barely fair. It rattled around and the fielder had a hard time tracking it down. Meanwhile, Jackson was running at full steam around third as the third base coach waved him around. Brad was not far being. Realizing the ball was going to stay in the park, he had gotten on his horse and was blazing around second as fast as he could go. He looked up at the third base coach who was frantically winding his arm. Brad rounded third as the left fielder got to the ball, pivoted and fired it towards the infield.

Brad came around third and spotted the 17 inch wide 5-sided plate. Ninety feet! He would cover the ground in less than three seconds, and history would be his. He saw Freeman set up, blocking the plate, to receive the throw that Brad knew would be coming. He took the first step around third and felt it, a tightening in his chest so severe, he straightened up. He nearly stumbled as he grabbed at his chest with both hands, trying to squash the pain, stifle the intensity. He stumbled and took two more steps before doing a full cartwheel and landing on his back, 10 feet from home plate. Marisa screamed and jumped out of her first row seat and ran onto the field. Sparky Freeman caught the relay from the shortstop and just stood at home plate staring in disbelief at Brad lying on the ground, gasping for air. Brad's teammates momentarily stopped when Brad started to cartwheel, but now as a group, they rushed onto the field.

Marisa got to him first. Brad was not moving save for the heaving in his chest. She dropped to the ground and gently lifted his head up in her hands. His teammates soon arrived and stopped, surrounding the motionless Brad. She rubbed his brow and rocked his head in her arms. Brad looked into her eyes, and slowly raised his head. He turned, looking at the plate then up at Sparky holding the ball in his bare right hand. With all his effort, he placed his hands on the ground behind him and lifted his weight until he could twist and plant his knees. He began to crawl toward home as his teammates, Marisa, and 40 thousand faithful looked on in disbelief. As he neared the catcher, he looked up into his eyes and said, "Sparky, you have a choice to make."

Freeman looked down at the ailing superstar crawling towards him. Brad was one of his idols growing up. He knew all of Brad's stats and had even been able to see him a few times at Tiger stadium, making the trip from his home town of Lansing several times with his dad. He was well aware of the controversy surrounding Brad these past few weeks and felt sorry and concerned for him. But that was that and this was now. Sparky had one thing to do, and that was to get the out.

Garcia, who had been positioned behind Freeman to back up the play, was yelling at his catcher to make the tag. The other infielders began running toward the plate, also yelling at him to tag Brad out.

Sparky looked at the ball in his bare hand and began to lean forward with his right arm, but stopped. He looked ahead at Marisa, still kneeling on the third base line, up at the crowd, over to his screaming teammates, then down at Brad. He tossed the ball aside, bent down and helped Brad to his feet and walked with him to home plate, where Brad unsteadily touched his right foot to the rubber pentagon as the crowd erupted.

Made in the USA
San Bernardino, CA
24 November 2015